the
Great
Good
Summer

Praise for
The Great Good Summer

One of Kate DiCamillo's summer reading
picks in *Time for Kids* magazine

★ "This engaging debut novel hooks readers from beginning to
end. . . . This tender and funny story of a strong-willed young girl is
reminiscent of Rita Williams-Garcia's *One Crazy Summer* and Kate
DiCamillo's *Because of Winn-Dixie*."

—*School Library Journal*, starred review

★ "Readers will be rewarded with both genuine adventure and
intense reflection as Ivy finds a balance between safe comfort and
disquieting wonder."

—*Publishers Weekly*, starred review

"Ivy's quirky voice narrates the story, which is full of adventure, to
be sure, but also meditations on home, family, and the differences—
and striking similarities—between science and religion. . . . Equal
parts peculiar and poignant, Ivy's story will have readers giggling as
they root for her to find everything she's looking for."

—*Kirkus Reviews*

"Ivy is a delicious character with a smart, believable voice. The
conversations between churchgoing Ivy and science-loving Paul

are some of the best parts of the book. . . . Give this to readers who like their coming-of-age journeys with a hint of religion and a dose of humor."

—*Booklist*

"It's a rare book that can discuss faith without verging into the preachy and contemplat[e] the nature of God while acknowledging some people's lack of belief—all in the voice of an earnest, honest twelve-year-old girl. Scanlon manages it in this story. . . . Heartfelt in content and authentic in tone, this will resonate with kids questioning their parents, God, or both."

—*Bulletin of the Center for Children's Books*

"I loved this book for Ivy's tenderness and strength, for her so-real voice. I loved it for Ivy and Paul's growing friendship and what this says about true love. Liz Garton Scanlon has, with courage and tons of artistry, given us a fun and suspenseful story that is not afraid to ask the big questions."

—Francisco X. Stork, author of *Marcelo in the Real World*

"When Ivy Green can't take any more missing, when even God seems to have taken off for parts unknown (along with her mama), redemption nevertheless appears—in the sky, the stars, a kind-of-cute science boy, and a whole cast of people who love her. Liz Garton Scanlon has written a great-good miracle of a book. I can't stop hugging it."

—Kathi Appelt, author of *The Underneath*

The Great Sum

BEACH LANE BOOKS

New York   London   Toronto   Sydney   New Delhi

Good

LIZ GARTON SCANLON

mer

Beach Lane Books
An imprint of Simon & Schuster Children's Publishing Division
1230 Avenue of the Americas, New York, New York 10020
This book is a work of fiction. Any references to historical events, real people, or real places are used fictitiously. Other names, characters, places, and events are products of the author's imagination, and any resemblance to actual events or places or persons, living or dead, is entirely coincidental.
Text copyright © 2015 by Liz Garton Scanlon
Cover illustration copyright © 2015 by Marla Frazee
All rights reserved, including the right of reproduction in whole or in part in any form.
BEACH LANE BOOKS is a trademark of Simon & Schuster, Inc.
For information about special discounts for bulk purchases, please contact Simon & Schuster Special Sales at 1-866-506-1949 or business@simonandschuster.com.
The Simon & Schuster Speakers Bureau can bring authors to your live event. For more information or to book an event, contact the Simon & Schuster Speakers Bureau at 1-866-248-3049 or visit our website at www.simonspeakers.com.
Also available in a Beach Lane Books hardcover edition
Book design by Lauren Rille
The text for this book was set in Fairfield Lt Std.
Manufactured in the United States of America
0416 OFF
First Beach Lane Books paperback edition May 2016
10 9 8 7 6 5 4 3 2 1
The Library of Congress has cataloged the hardcover edition as follows:
Scanlon, Elizabeth Garton.
The great good summer / Liz Garton Scanlon.—First edition.
p. cm.
Summary: Loomer, Texas, twelve-year-old Ivy Green, whose mother may have run off with a charismatic preacher to Panhandle, Florida, and classmate Paul Dobbs, who wants to see a Space Shuttle before the program is scrapped, team up for a summer adventure that is full of surprises.
ISBN 978-1-4814-1147-9 (hardcover)
ISBN 978-1-4814-1149-3 (eBook)
[1. Runaways—Fiction. 2. Bus travel—Fiction. 3. Christian life—Fiction. 4. Mothers and daughters—Fiction. 5. Friendship—Fiction.] I. Title.
PZ7.S2798Gre 2015
[Fic]—dc23
2014014988
ISBN 978-1-4814-1148-6 (pbk)

For Lynn, Carrie, Kathie,
Shannon, Bern, and Barbara—
Oh My Goodness!

the Great Good Summer

Chapter One

God is alive and well in Loomer, Texas, so I don't know why Mama had to go all the way to The Great Good Bible Church of Panhandle Florida to find him, or to find herself, either.

Daddy says she went to get some of the sadness out of her system. He says it like it should be as easy as getting a soda stain out of a skirt. A little scrub, a little soak, one quick run through the machine—good as new and no big deal.

Every day since Mama left, Daddy's been trying to convince me that things aren't all that bad, even though Mama's become a Holy Roller and has disappeared with a preacher who calls himself Hallelujah Dave.

Meanwhile I've been trying to convince Daddy that things *are* truly and indeed all that bad. Hallelujah Dave, for goodness' sake.

"I promise I'm not just being sassy, Daddy, but explain to me again how lying around on the ground speaking in tongues is gonna get anything out of Mama's system?"

"We don't know that she's really lying on the ground, baby," says Daddy. Which, you have to admit, is a minor quibble. And you'll notice, he doesn't mention the speaking in tongues. What he *does* do is pour me a big bowl of puffed rice and hand me a banana from across our kitchen table.

For my whole life Mama's always cooked breakfast—something hot, like eggs or oatmeal—but I don't mention that 'cause it's not Daddy's fault that we're here all alone with cold cereal, no eggs, and no Mama-in-her-own-mama's-apron. It's not his fault, but I'm not used to this way of doing things, and I don't really want to be.

Until the wildfires in the spring, everything was perfectly great-good enough here at home in Loomer. I mean, we've got more churches than Quik Marts. Way more. And we have Advent Oil and Lube, and we have Heaven Sent Hair Designs, and we have Creation Concrete. And we pray in school, which the science club doesn't like, but that doesn't seem to stop anybody except the kids in science club. We have all that godliness, but we don't have The Great Good Bible Church.

Apparently those fires just freaked her all the way out and she needed help to make sense of it all. Or at least that's what she said ten days ago when she actually up and left.

"I need to see the truth and be the truth," said Mama, "and Hallelujah Dave says The Great Good Bible Church is the place to do that. You understand."

But we didn't.

My mouth partly filled with cereal, I say, "Daddy, she's been gone long enough to have called us, though, right? And she hasn't yet. So are you gonna do anything about that?" I reach my wet spoon into the sugar bowl and pull a big scoop back onto the cardboardy puffs getting soggy in my bowl.

"Ivy-girl, I don't think there's a dang thing more I *can* do, 'cept let your mama get right with God. We're here, safe and sound, and she'll be back soon. And in the meantime, I may not be a mother, but I can take care of my daughter. Nobody's gonna tell me I can't."

And with that, he pushes back his chair, sets his coffee cup down just a little bit too loudly in the sink, and slips his Green's Roofing ball cap onto his head. I can tell by the clock above the stove that he doesn't really need to leave for work quite yet, but he is obviously done with this conversation, so I guess I am too.

I want to say, "How do you *know* she'll be back soon?"

but instead I say, "You're doing a fine job, Daddy," and I mean it. He's doing as best he can. And the least I can do is put up the breakfast dishes and make the beds and maybe even run a load of dirty clothes without complaining.

"You too. Love you, baby," Daddy says, and then he sighs and shakes his head and walks out the door.

Here's something that's not very good about The Great Good Bible Church of Panhandle Florida. It's in Florida.

And here's another thing: it doesn't have a website. It doesn't have an address or a phone number or ratings or reviews or anything. It's almost like it doesn't really exist. And for all we know about Hallelujah Dave, he might as well be a bogeyman or something who swept Mama off into the swamps of Florida, never to be seen again.

When I say as much to Daddy, he says, "Your mama's too smart to fall for a bogeyman, Ivy. We've got to have faith in that." Which isn't super-reassuring, if you ask me.

If Mama were here, she'd say, "Ivy, don't be flat-out ridiculous. You let your imagination run away from you like a fox with a ham hock. Keep your head on, honey, and say a prayer that God doesn't get a look at your crazy ideas and make them all come true." Because she's practical that way.

But the thing is, ideas are my talent. My only talent, really. My voice isn't right for singing, I freeze up in the spelling bee, and I can't shoot a basket to save my life. If I stop coming up with ideas, I'm not gonna have anything left to do or talk about.

This year in English class Mrs. Murray asked us to create a motto, and mine was, "Every good day starts with an idea." Mrs. Murray liked it. She said it was not just a motto but an *inspirational* motto. And Paul Dobbs, who was my tablemate in English but who'd barely ever whispered a word to me, said, "Yeah, that's cool. It's kind of like saying 'Every good experiment begins with a hypothesis,' isn't it? I might change my motto!" Which goes down in history as the first and only time I've ever said anything even mildly impressive to an egghead like Paul Dobbs.

At home when I showed my motto to Mama, she said, "Yes, every good day starts with an idea. That may be true. But not all *ideas* are good."

Considering where Mama is or isn't right this very moment, I could say the same to her.

This is the second summer in a row that Mrs. Murray's hired me to help take care of Devon and Lucy. Maybe she hired me on account of my ideas. Or maybe it's because I live on the same side of town, and I get good grades, and she knows my mama and daddy. She trusts me. But if I don't leave the house right now, I'll prove her wrong, because I'm never gonna get there by nine o'clock.

I put my lock and chain and a can of orange soda in my backpack, and I jump on my bike, sidesaddle. Rolling down the alley behind my house, I slip past the Larsons' backyard and the Melroys' and the Newtons'—and there are Abby Newton and Kimmy Roy, sitting on the bench by the Newtons' garage, painting their toenails and tossing a ball for Abby's dog. Because of course Abby's lucky enough to have a dog. (Personally, I think if you're an only child, you should automatically be issued a dog when you're born, as a consolation prize, but my mama and daddy disagree.)

"Hey, Abby. Hey, Kimmy. Hey, Buddy," I say, but I keep moving so I don't have to get into a big conversation, since everything with Abby and Kimmy—especially Kimmy—is a big conversation.

"Hey, Ivy!" Abby yells when she sees me.

"Hey, Ivy!" echoes Kimmy. "Abby says your mom went to, like, seminary or some kind of crazy God camp or something? For the summer? Is that true?"

I'm still sidesaddle, with only my left butt cheek on the seat, so I whip my left leg all the way over the center bar of my bright blue bike and start pedaling in earnest. "Yep. Something like that," I say, and I keep pedaling, faster and faster, to get away from them and from the honest truth about my mother.

$\mathcal{M}$ ama thinks Mrs. Murray is kind of kooky. That's what Mama calls people who aren't originally from Loomer, or who dress a little differently than she does, or who don't go to Second Baptist.

But Mrs. Murray gets the *Loomer Press* delivered every day, and she has pots of blue hydrangeas on her stoop, and pretty pottery wind chimes and a welcome mat. She's a teacher and a mother and a volleyball coach, *and* she writes novels in the summer, on a cute laptop with a rainbowy cover. She has a husband and two kids and a little red car. If you ask me, everything about Mrs. Murray is as normal as normal can be.

And, not to point fingers or anything, but nobody at the Murray house followed a perfect stranger to Florida for the summer, if you know what I mean.

I roll my bike into the Murrays' garage, my pulse still pounding and my head thrumming with things I might've said to Abby and Kimmy about Mama. Things like, "Yeah, she's bleeding out of her hands and feet like Jesus, and her head spins around like in that old movie where the girl gets possessed." Or, "She went off to pray that you guys don't go to hell for painting your fingernails blue and triple-piercing your ears." Or, "God told her to start a mega-church on a riverboat in Louisiana, and we're gonna be millionaires by Christmas."

But I didn't say those things, because even when I'm worried and frustrated and running late, I'm not much of a liar. And the truth would have either gotten them talking about me to the other girls at school or made them feel sorry for me in kind of a pathetic way, or both. That's why I rode on.

'Cause here's what really happened: after the forest fires burnt down what seemed like half of Texas—including the old wooden church where Mama's daddy was the preacher when she was a girl—Mama went down to the Red Cross to volunteer. I don't know what she thought she'd be able to do, but it turned out not much. I mean, she sorted some canned goods and she made a delivery of clothes from our church and she helped out for a couple of days at the shelter that they'd set up at one of the high schools. But buildings had been burned and ranches ruined, and blackened trees stood still as skeletons. There really wasn't a thing *anyone* could do, at least not about any of that.

So after a week of helping out where she could, Mama came home wringing her hands and saying, "I'd like to see God explain *this*. I'd just like for him to really and truly help me understand *this*!"

She said it over and over again and then she went to bed and stayed there, for six straight days. Which meant she missed my end-of-year ceremony at school—never mind that my mama never misses a single thing and, also, she was supposed to be in charge of refreshments. Daddy had to call Mrs. Luck and have her reassign the job because Mama "wasn't feeling well." That's what he said, like it was just that simple.

Meanwhile, I didn't understand what Mama was feeling or doing any better than she understood the fires that had left gray ash floating through the air around us, like some sort of ghostly confetti. She had never acted anything like this, not one day in my whole life.

"It is a mystery," said Daddy when I tried to get him to explain it to me. "But, baby, everybody gets a little down every now and then. She just needs rest." And then he put his finger up to his lips to remind me to be quiet—for the sixth day in a row.

When she finally got up out of bed, it was to go for groceries. But instead of buying milk and eggs, she found a flyer about a new ministry in town, set up for the very purpose of healing hearts after the fires. And I guess she went straight there and started speaking in tongues, of all things.

It wasn't even Mama who told us about it. Her friend Carlene, from church, was over at the strip mall getting a bikini wax. (I'm not gossiping—she included that as part of her story, which I kind of could not believe. Carlene is the least likely person in the world to wear a bikini, honestly.) Anyway, there were these big double doors, wide open to the sunshine, right next to the waxing studio, and Carlene specifically noticed them because they'd always been locked up tight with a FOR LEASE sign on them, for as long as she'd been going over there. So she couldn't hardly help but look to see what was going on.

"And there was a young man preaching like the gates to hell were just around the corner," she said, and people kneeling and keening and lying on the ground moaning and speaking the language of Babel. "I couldn't stop looking, I admit it," she said, which is how she came to realize that one of the moaners was Mama. Carlene drove straight to our house to tell us, because she knew we'd need to know. That's how she put it, like she was doing us a huge favor.

"Don't tell your mama, but I've always thought Carlene was sort of a busybody," said Daddy when she left. And then he dropped his head into his hands and rubbed his scalp, hard.

That night Daddy asked Mama about the preacher at the strip mall. Her hair was sort of wild like she was still on her six days in bed, but her eyes were shiny and wide awake. "He appeared in Loomer to save me. The answer to my prayers," she said. "If that's not a miracle . . ."

I don't think the whole thing makes any more sense to Daddy than it does to me, even though he's acting like it's temporary and all under control. He just doesn't go in for drama. Here's the thing, though—neither does Mama, usually. Whenever somebody in Loomer does something a little different, like skydiving or breaking off an engagement or something, Mama shrugs and says, "Seems a little kooky to me, but what do I know? You know me, Miss Straight-and-Narrow."

I don't know what really happened to Mama, deep down, during those wildfires, but I can tell you that Miss Straight-and-Narrow would not have gone to bed for six days, she would not have gone down to a creepy church in a strip mall, and she most definitely would not have

gone off to Florida ten days later with a preacher called
Hallelujah Dave.

"Happy summer, sweet Ivy," says Mrs. Murray when she
opens the door. "Hurry on in. I've only been home from
school for a week, and I've about lost my marbles already.
But it's absolutely beautiful out, and ohmygoodness, I'm
burning with ideas and ready to write! Remember your
motto about good ideas? Well, I've got some, and I plan
to use them! I think you and Lucy and Devon should go
to the park on this pretty day, and I'll stay here and make
something of myself. Yes?"

Mrs. Murray often talks in big rushy streams like
this. Last year a couple of kids started a petition saying
they wanted her to put an outline on the board every day
because it was hard to take notes when she was always
talking around and around in circles. I didn't sign it. I
thought, *Well, if it's hard to take notes, don't take them.
Just listen.*

"Yes," I say. "The park. That'll be really nice. And that's
great about your ideas!"

I hope I'll be a little bit like Mrs. Murray when I grow
up. She actually *does* something with her ideas instead of
just think them.

I follow her through the front door and straight into the living room. Right there in front of me sit Devon and Lucy and their blocks and books and breakfast dishes. Lucy comes running over before I'm even all the way through the door, looking up at me with her cute, pink little smile but grabbing on to her mama's leg at the same time.

"Lucy! It's summer! I've missed you, you little pip. You're always sleeping when I babysit during the school year." I lean down to touch her face, but she turns in toward Mrs. Murray's leg, so I let her be. Last summer she'd just barely turned one, so I'm sure she really doesn't remember me at all.

Mrs. Murray backs into the house with Lucy still attached to her knee and says, "Let's pack a bag for y'all, with snacks and such, right? And, Ivy, tell me about your mama, honey. Your daddy's doing a roof for Mr. Dolan and told him your mama went away for the summer?"

Which I guess means it's public, Mama's taking off. I mean if Abby and Kimmy know, and Mr. Dolan and Mrs. Murray know, and Daddy's talking about it as if Mama's taken off to Paris for a holiday or something, then it must be public.

"She did. I mean, I guess she did. We don't really

know exactly how long she'll be gone, I guess." I don't know what else to say, unless I go into the part about my granddaddy's church burning down and Mama's freaking out and the six days in bed and all. Right now just doesn't seem the time.

So instead I say, "She's at church." Which sounds really funny, since normally if you go to church, you would go for, like, an hour or two. Not for a whole summer.

"Well. I'll bet you're going to miss her, huh?" Mrs. Murray says, and I just nod, because a knot of tears suddenly sticks in the back of my throat and makes it so I can't talk.

Yes, I think. *Yes, I'm going to miss her.*

I guess that's what I've been trying to tell Daddy since she left. And, now that I think of it, ever since the fires in the spring. The fires that left behind black trees and charcoaly rubble and some sort of hole in my mama's heart. Yes. I just plain miss Mama.

I lean up against the counter next to Mrs. Murray and the snacks and the apple juice, and I think about my mama in our kitchen—how she's always been there every day of my whole entire life and now she's not.

And then I help Mrs. Murray bag up the little crackers and chunks of pear without saying another word. She fills the sippy cups, grabs a stack of clean, dry clothes—just in case—and helps me shove everything into my pack. When we're all set, she grabs Lucy and I grab Devon and we step back outside and plop them in their double stroller, which is the size, I promise you, of a small train.

"Kisses, little Luce," Mrs. Murray says to Lucy, and then plants a kiss on the top of Lucy's head. "Kisses, Devon-bo-beven," she says to Devon, with the same kiss for him.

"And thank you, Ivy," she says to me. "You're an angel." And I know she doesn't mean it in a churchy or mysterious way at all. She just means I'm helping out.

East Loomer Park is kind of fancy. It wasn't when I was little, but a couple of years ago there was some big pile of money from an election or something, and now it's all city-slickered up. That's what Daddy calls it—city-slickered up, and fancy. It's where all of Loomer goes when the mayor gives a speech or someone's hosting a fundraiser or a family wants to have a big birthday party with a bouncy house.

There is a red stone track around the pond for people to jog on, and there're two playgrounds—one for babies and one for big kids—with brand-new, bright-colored plastic equipment. And there's a dog park and a few gardens and a whole bunch of other stuff.

"Do ya want me to push you guys high?" I ask Lucy and Devon as we come up on the swings.

"No," says Lucy.

"Do ya want to play in the sand?" I ask when we get to the dinosaur dig.

"No," says Devon.

"Do ya want a snack?" I ask at Picnic Hill, with its tables and shade trees and thick green grass.

"No snack at all," Lucy says, and even though I'm getting a little tired of them saying no to all of my ideas, I'm kind of impressed by Lucy's sentence.

"Good talking, Luce!" I say.

On the other side of Picnic Hill is the skate park where all the rough boys go to do fancy tricks in the big concrete scoop. There are three high schoolers there today. One of them I know for sure is Jenny Abler's older brother, and one of the others is this boy called Jake who Abby had kind of a crush on for a while even though he's never given her the time of day, and I'm pretty sure her parents would completely disapprove of him due to his long hair and baggy pants and extreme oldness. But these days Abby's not really into her parents or the things her

parents approve of. Which personally makes me a tidge nervous, but I guess that's why I'm not Abby.

Just past the skate park is the fenced area that's for remote controlled airplanes and helicopters and stuff, and it turns out that *this* is what the Murray babies want to do today—watch the planes. They want to sit pressed against the fence and stare up at the sky. So we do.

We sit for maybe fifteen minutes, looking and oohing and aahing as the planes make big loops in the sky. Then suddenly I feel someone standing right behind me.

"Hey, Ivy," a voice says, and when I turn around, there are Dash Bauer and Paul Dobbs, from school. "Looks like you've been cloned," says Dash, shrugging at the babies.

"Twice," says Paul. And they laugh.

I've never actually noticed that the Murray babies look a little bit like me, at least as much as everyone with light brown hair and light brown eyes and pinkish skin looks a little alike. I mean, I guess that's what Dash and Paul are getting at.

"Yeah, right," I say. "Since cloning is legal and possible and all."

Lucy and Devon stare up at the boys, wide eyed. Lucy grabs on to my leg, just the way she did with Mrs. Murray, but Devon points at Paul.

"Airplane!" he says.

"Ha. You've got good taste," says Paul. He smiles sort of a half smile and bends down to show Devon what he's got in his hands. It's a slick-looking black-and-red-and-silver jet, with fins and a domed window. And there's at least one other plane, plus a bunch of antennae and stuff sticking out of the bag at Paul's feet. "We're gonna fly 'em," Paul says to Devon. "Wanna watch?"

"Sure, we'll watch. Right, guys?" I say, flat-out relieved that we've moved on from the cloning jokes.

I don't know what to say around the science guys. I never have. They aren't scary in that way the super-popular kids are—you're not gonna get tripped in the hall or laughed at during a pep rally or anything—but they sort of speak their own language, and it's pretty impossible to understand. I'm not saying I'm dumb. I've been on the honor roll since the third grade, which is when we first got letter grades. But I'm mostly smart about reading and writing, and the science guys are smart about how the world works. Or at least how they *think* the world works.

Paul and Dash push through the swinging gate and start setting out their equipment—airplanes and a helicopter and remote controls and a round red target they lay out on the ground in front of them. And big bottles of bright blue power drink and bags of chips. They greet the folks already flying with handshakes and fist bumps—they all seem to know each other—and right then, before Paul's plane is even up, Lucy says, "Potty. Go potty now."

"Do you wanna watch the flying first, Lucy?" I say, but she's already up on her feet, reaching for my fingers.

"Go potty. Now." She actually looks a little desperate.

"Okay, guys. Let's head over to the bathroom," I say, hopping up quickly and bending down to swoop them up. But that's when Devon starts to scream. He screams, "No, no, no, no, no," and he makes his body stiff and heavy. He always seems so much older than Lucy, but really he's just a little three-year-old himself.

"Devon, help me out here. Lucy's got to go. Will you help me, buddy?" But he can't hear me for all his screaming, and then Lucy starts to cry too—hard, till her face is bright pink and puffy.

"Ivy, do you need help?" Paul's looking at us through the fence, his hands hanging limply at his sides, flying gear in each one.

I look up at him to make certain he's not laughing at me, before I say, "No, I don't think so." Not because I don't need help but because I don't know what on

20

God's green earth I would ask him to do. I have two crying babies and a stroller the size of a small train, and in between every cry all I can hear is the model planes whirring a noisy, endless whir.

It's hardly a wonder that as I partly push, partly drag the stroller and the babies toward the bathroom on the other side of Picnic Hill, the knot of tears pops back into my throat.

By the time we've made it all the way to the bathroom—but too late—and changed Lucy's clothes and calmed everyone down and wiped noses and repacked the bag, I just don't have it in me to hoof back over to the airspace.

"We're near the dog park," I say. "Wanna have a snack and watch the dogs?"

And to my deep, deep relief, both Lucy and Devon say yes.

I'm pretty sure I prefer dogs to flying machines anyway.

Chapter Three

*M*orning comes in, all pink, through the lacy layers of my curtains and lands like a sunburn on my skin. I roll away from the light and think, *It is summer, and Mama has gone to The Great Good Bible Church of Panhandle Florida, and I'm gonna have cold cereal for breakfast again.*

And then I think, *I'm gonna be sad but I'll pretend I'm not sad, and Daddy's gonna be sad but he'll pretend he's not sad. That's all we can really do for each other these days.*

And *then* I think, *Today is Sunday, and Daddy's gonna make us go to church for the first time since Mama left two weeks ago.* "We can't avoid it forever," he said last night, even while I was thinking, *Oh, yes we can. We should.*

Once I'm dressed in a sundress and a shrug and sandals—sandals that are hand-me-downs from Mama—I wander downstairs. Daddy hurries us through our breakfast as if he's actually excited to get to church. I am not excited. I would be happier doing pretty much anything else. Honestly, at this moment I would rather go to the dentist than go to church, and that's saying something.

(I hate the dentist because I always, without fail, have a cavity. Mama says it's not my fault—that I have soft teeth, teeth like loam, just like she did as a little girl—but the reason doesn't matter when the dentist gets his drill out. It hurts every time. But then, when he's done, I feel fine. I feel better, actually.)

This is different. I just know that church isn't gonna fix up any holes in me today.

"Ivy-girl, you're dawdling," says Daddy. "Church doesn't wait on its sheep, sweetheart."

"Daddy, what are we gonna say when people ask us about Mama?" I stir my bowl of milk. Daddy's right. I'm dawdling.

"The truth, baby. They're church folks. Church folks understand other church folks."

I follow Daddy out the kitchen door into the garage. "This thing with Mama is churchier than church, though. Right? Isn't that the problem?"

Daddy doesn't answer me for a second because he's getting settled in his seat and looking around—at my bike on one side and mama's car on the other. Mama's car just sitting there, all locked up in the hot and dark. Once he's started up the car and pushed the button to roll the garage door up, he says, "Actually the opposite. I don't know that this guy is offering your mother much church at all." He reaches around my seat and turns to look out the back window as he pulls out. His lips are pulled tight and white, and the car jerks because he speeds up too quickly.

"What do you mean, Daddy? Do you know something that you haven't told me?" If I was 100 percent nervous five minutes ago, now I'm double that.

"You can't believe how little I know," he says with kind of a harsh little chuckle. It's scary.

And then suddenly everything changes back. It's like he's in a play and he's just switched roles from the mad dad character to a jollier, more familiar one. "I was thinking we'd go out for Sunday burgers after worship," he says. "You wanna do that, Ives? Sunday burgers and chocolate shakes?" Daddy knows I can't say no to Snow's chocolate shakes, so I guess he's got me there. I can't argue or ask another thing after that, so I sit worrying, quiet as a mouse, till we pull up to Second Baptist.

Pastor Lou greets us in the open door of the sanctuary. "Well, if it isn't Ivy Green and her daddy, Maxwell," he says. "I am mighty happy to see the two of you today." Which might be what he says to each of us every Sunday, but today it sounds fishy, like he's saying, "It's hard to believe you're here, considering the fact that your wife-slash-mama's gone off half-cocked crazy and the two of you are home alone living on cold cereal and soda pop."

I like Pastor Lou well enough, I guess, but honestly, it'd be nice if he didn't always have to comment on who we are and what we do. Mama says that's a preacher's job—to be God's eyes down here on earth. But don't you think sometimes a person can see well enough for herself what's going on, without a preacher's summary of the whole thing?

We file on in, saying our hellos and settling into our usual pew near the Loomises, and then we run through the first set of hymns.

"Would you bless our homes and families . . . ," we sing.

"Help us learn to love each other with a love that constant stays . . ."

I try to follow along—verse one, then two, then four—the way we're supposed to, but I can't resist. I peek straight away at verse three, the bit we skip every time. Mama says we leave it out to leave room for God, which is the same reason she and Daddy didn't give me a middle name.

"We could've come up with something," said Mama

one of the five thousand times I asked her why I wasn't Ivy Anne or Ivy Marie or something. "We could've come up with something, but what could possibly be better than leaving an open window for God," she said, "right in the middle of your name?"

If "God is in everyone and everything," which is what the marquee out in front of the church said last time I looked, an open window seems like overkill to me, and I can think of a lot of things I'd like better. But never mind, because here I sit, Ivy Blank Green, whispering verse three, "From the homes in which we're nurtured, with the love that shapes us there . . . ," knowing deep down that those words belong in the song, just like my missing middle name belongs to me.

The offering baskets move from row to row, and as they fill up with bright white envelopes, folks call out prayers, first for everyone who's been impacted by the fires—the ones who've lost their homes and all their treasures, the ones who may not have a school to go to in the fall. This is how our services have opened up ever since spring, and it really *is* a sorrow that there is still so much to pray for. Say what you will about Mama, but she was right about that.

Then we move on to pray for people from our own

congregation—Louise Schmitt, who's in the hospital; and Riley Cole, who's overseas with the navy risking life and limb; and Darryl Rhodes, who was already dealing with a bad divorce and bankruptcy, but now he's gonna have to rebuild his barns after the fires too. (His sister Sharlene doesn't say all this when she offers up the prayer, because that'd be cruel and a little gossipy. Plus, everyone knows it all anyway. She just asks that we "pray for my dear brother Darryl in his suffering.")

Then, with no warning to me at all, Daddy calls one out for Mama.

"Please say a prayer for our Diana, who is traveling in the name of God," says Daddy, and everyone says, "Let it be so."

"Lord have mercy," I whisper. Not for Mama but for me—mortified, blushing, no-middle-name me. I look down at Mama's shoes and wish, more than anything, that she were here to wear them.

And then, as if he'd been waiting all morning for us to call attention to ourselves, Pastor Lou launches into his sermon.

"Today we look at the book of Ruth, from the Old Testament," he says, "and we ponder faith and constancy. We think about Naomi and about Ruth, and about how their loyalty to home and family is the most important lesson we are given by strong biblical woman. It's an old familiar story, but here's the important part . . ." He pauses and, I swear, looks right at me when he does. Like, he meets my eyes. It's creepy.

"In Naomi's darkest hour," he says, "when she is in another land and has lost everything there is to lose, she yearns for home. It is in a person's moral fiber to want home—a woman's, in particular."

A few folks mutter, "Amen."

"And Naomi's daughter-in-law Ruth? What does Ruth do? She comforts Naomi! She says, 'Your people shall be my people, and your God my God. Where you die, I will die, and there I will be buried.' What she means, brothers and sisters, is that she will demonstrate her faith in God *through* her faithfulness to family. In spite of everything," says Pastor Lou. "In spite of struggles, grief, and wildfires, there is faithfulness to family!"

"Amen, brother," mutter a few more folks. We are not a rowdy church. Once we get done singing hymns, muttering's about all we do. Granddaddy's church was full of "yellers and moaners," according to Mama, and she always thought that sort of spectacle was unnecessary. Until Hallelujah Dave came along, I guess.

Pastor Lou always says, "There's something for each of you in each of my words each week." But today it's sounding like every single word's just for us, for me and Daddy, whether we want them or not.

"And God rewards Ruth." He goes on, hardly even giving me a second to think, his words a little more like a song than a speech now, rolling up and down and up again. "He rewards her loyalty and steadiness with a good husband and a good life, and she is happy."

I shift in my seat so I can see Daddy out of the corner of my eye. Surely he thinks this whole thing is a little obvious, that good women are supposed to be faithful to their families above all? Through thick and thin? I mean, Pastor Lou's practically saying, "Loyal and steady, unlike *some* people I know!"

But Daddy just sits with his eyes closed and his hands folded in his lap, resting on the soft yellow newsletter bulletin we were handed on our way in. He just sits there not budging, as if Pastor Lou were reading the phone book or something.

Daddy is always the quietest, stillest church sitter on God's green earth. Mama says it's because his roofing job causes such a racket, he likes the peace of church. Personally, I wouldn't describe church as super-peaceful, what with all the lessons and prayers and instructions and amens. But since Mama's daddy was a fire-and-brimstone preacher in a yelling and moaning church, I guess she got to thinking of Pastor Lou as peaceful. And maybe compared to Granddaddy he is.

One time I asked Daddy what "fire-and-brimstone" meant, and he said, "Scoldings and warnings, mostly. Your granddaddy was big on scoldings and warnings." I never met Granddaddy, on account of him disowning Mama for marrying and having a baby so young. (That baby being me.) He died before he and Mama got a chance to make up. But I know enough to say that he sure didn't sound like much fun as a preacher or a daddy.

"Meanwhile," Pastor Lou goes on, "back in our present day, we've been rewarded with good lives too, brothers and sisters. But instead of being happy or grateful, we are led astray. We pull away. Even though our task, as modeled by Ruth, is to stick to our families like honeysuckle vine!"

Pastor Lou carries on, and the church gets hotter and hotter as he preaches. He somehow makes Job part of the story too, and Jesus and Matthew and the prodigal son. Honest to goodness, Pastor Lou can take twenty-five different bits of the Bible and make them all say the same thing if it suits him.

"My friends," he says, pretty loudly now but still sort of singing, "I'm here to affirm that sometimes our task in life isn't to *get* anywhere. It is to stay solid with the people we love. It is to promise, 'I will never leave you or forsake you.' We learn this, brothers and sisters, from God, from Jesus, and from Ruth."

And here's when I realize the worst part about Pastor Lou's sermon today. It's not for us—it's for Mama, and Mama's not here to hear a single word.

"I have to go to the restroom," I whisper to Daddy, and I slip out of our pew and tiptoe down the side aisle toward the back of the church. Kimmy and Kaitlyn Roy are sitting on the edge of the second-to-the-last row, playing hangman on the church bulletin, clear as day. Which Pastor Lou might call an abomination if he were paying any attention.

And I'm left to wondering why he doesn't focus on the "sinners in our midst"—that's what he calls us sometimes, the "sinners in our midst"—instead of the sinners holed up in The Great Good Bible Church of Panhandle Florida.

Chapter Four

"Well, what do you know? Ivy Green! I sure never thought I'd see the likes of you skipping out of church."

I would like to act either innocent or appalled, but it's true, I'm skipping out. When I came out of the ladies', I just couldn't make myself walk back down that aisle. Instead I tucked out the side door, thinking I'd sit on the cellar steps and kick stones around instead. But it turns out the cellar steps are taken up already by none other than Paul Dobbs, whom I haven't seen since Wednesday morning when the Murray babies and I had a meltdown in East Loomer Park.

"I'm not exactly skipping out, Paul-calling-the-kettle-black," I say, because you just know that Paul's mom and dad and sister, Jenny, are sitting in there, all fancy and proper while he skips out too. "It's just that I don't feel quite right," I say. "I needed a breath of air. And I'm pretty sure I can pray from out here," I say, like I'm kind of irritated with him, which for some reason I am.

"I'm pretty sure you can't," says Paul with a little twitch

of a smile as he scootches over to make room for me on the steps. "Pastor Lou thinks his God only looks after the folks inside Loomer Second Baptist Church, and preferably those in the front few pews like my family. He's got a stricter rubric than Mrs. Murray has for English papers, and if you don't follow it, you flunk straight out, no matter who you pray to."

I close my eyes and feel hot dots of sun, filtered through the leaves of the giant cedar elm, prick the skin on my face. My head starts to spin a little, and I realize I wasn't fibbing. I really don't feel well at all.

"Okay," I say as I open my eyes back up gently. "I'm sorry you're angry about the rules in both church and school, but I've got a headache, and I am not in the mood for a lecture. And by the way, I think Pastor Lou's God is the same God who looks after all of us."

I know it's a little hypocritical for me to be defending Pastor Lou right now, but the way Paul talks, it's like he knows better than all of us, including God. Which is what Daddy would call "high-and-mighty."

"Anyway," I say, "if you're so sure we're going straight to hell for sitting out back during service, what are you doing here instead of siting inside with your family in the front few rows?"

"Nope, you've got it wrong. *I* don't think we're going to hell. I'm just saying *Pastor Lou* will think we're going to hell. Here's a little news flash, Ivy. There is no hell, unless you count Loomer, Texas, in the summertime. And there's no heaven unless you mean the one Neil Armstrong and the boys got to fly through on their way to the moon. You can sit out here and try to get your prayers heard if you want, but I'm just killing time and looking for contrails."

I glance at Paul again. He's leaning back on his elbows, shirtsleeves rolled up, head tilted toward the sky.

"I don't know what you're talking about," I say. "I don't see a thing up there, not a cricket or a crow. Maybe God's hiding the contrails from you since you basically just said he doesn't exist, which I'm pretty sure is sacrilegious, especially if you're on church property when you say it."

"Do y'know," says Paul, "that later this summer, one of the space shuttles is gonna fly over Loomer? We'll probably be able to see it from right here on these steps if we want to."

Paul can apparently change subjects just as quick as Daddy.

"The real space shuttle? Doesn't the space shuttle go

up? Into space? Why would anyone fly a rocket ship over Loomer?"

And here's where I should be getting the nervous willies, because church will be letting out soon and I am gonna have to explain myself. And explaining may well entail lying, which isn't exactly recommended at Second Baptist. Plus, I seem to be stuck in the middle of a conversation with one of the top eggheads in school, and no good can come of that, that's for sure.

I close my eyes and feel the sun prick my skin again.

"Well, first off, y'know it's not a rocket ship, right?" says Paul.

My eyes slide back open, and I turn to look at him. Here we go with the science.

"It's a spacecraft," he says. "And there's actually more than one of them, even though we call them all 'the space shuttle.'" Paul does finger quotes around the words "the space shuttle" as he speaks.

"But, yeah. Other than that, you're right. It *should* be going up to where it's built to go—space. Instead, the politicians have decided that we're done with all that, no more space shuttle. Before most of us even got a chance to be a part of the whole deal. So they're strapping one of 'em onto an airplane and flying it to Los Angeles and puttin' it up in a museum forever and ever. Amen, as y'all would say."

"Oh. Well, that's too bad," I answer, because I hear an ache in Paul's voice that makes me feel a little sorry, even though I'm not totally sure why. When I turn toward him, he's looking down, like he's given up on finding contrails or anything else in the sky. "But a museum's nice, right?" I say. "So lots of folks can see it?"

Paul stands up and shakes out his pants and stretches his arms above his head, like he's just waking up. "Ha," he says, in this really sarcastic way. "You sound just like my mom. I'm sure both of you mean well, but a museum means it's history. Over and done with," he says. "The end of curiosity and exploration and discovery, not only for guys like me who thought we'd hitch a ride to the International Space Station someday, but for everyone. I mean, I guess they'll keep sending unmanned spacecraft out there—y'know, rovers and stuff—but sometimes you've gotta go somewhere in person to understand it, right? You can't just plant yourself in a place like Loomer for the rest of your life and expect to learn anything."

And right then Paul Dobbs turns around and walks straight up the cellar steps, across the sidewalk, and out past the big cedar elm. He keeps walking through the hot paved parking lot of Loomer Second Baptist Church and turns left onto Allen Avenue. He doesn't look back, not once, and he doesn't look like he plans to stay planted anywhere.

Chapter Five

So here's when I know for certain that things with Mama have gone all kinds of wrong. We're sitting at Snow Drugstore, sipping our after-church shakes, and Donnetta Snow steps over from the pharmacy counter to say hi.

"Max, Ivy," she says. "Best chocolate shakes this side of Houston?"

"Well, hello, Donnetta," says Daddy. "Good to see you. And yep, they're as good as ever. My little Ivy-girl was suffering a bit of heatstroke after church, and a chocolate shake seems to be the cure-all!" Daddy winks at me, and Donnetta smiles her famous Donnetta Snow smile. I sip my shake and feel relieved I've been forgiven for ducking out of church. Daddy hardly seemed to mind at all, which makes me think he's been feeling sorrier for me than he's let on.

"Aw, I'm glad, honey," Donnetta says, and she ruffles my hair so that my skin tingles. In a good way.

"Now, Max," she says, "I've been meaning to call you to ask what you want me to do with Diana's prescriptions. She hasn't picked them up, and I understand she's out of town, but if my calculations are correct, she's run out of two of them. Are you sending things to her?"

I suck up a quick, nervous straw full of ice cream, and it goes straightaway to my brain and gives me a freeze headache. So much for a milk shake being a cure-all.

Mama *needs* her pills. She always has. She has high blood pressure from her daddy and something she calls "swell finger" from her mama, and she never, ever misses a single day of her pills. But then she's never missed any of my school events before this year's end-of-year ceremony either.

"Well, that," says Daddy, "is a very good question, Donnetta."

And then he looks at me like *I* might know what to do about Mama or her pills or Donnetta Snow. He looks at me like he's got no idea what to do about any of it himself. He looks at me like he's afraid. Afraid that Mama's not of her right mind. Or that Hallelujah Dave isn't. Or that we may never get Mama back home with us in Loomer, Texas, where she belongs.

And I decide right then and there that there's hardly a thing worse in the world than seeing your own daddy look that afraid.

In the car Daddy says nothing. He buckles up and sets the bag with Mama's pills on the seat between us, and he drives. His lips are tight and white again, and I can tell he doesn't want to talk, but I do. So I say, "Daddy, Mama thinks all the best conversations happen in the car." Y'know, sort of as a hint. But he doesn't take it that way. At all.

He stops super-suddenly at the four-way stop near Kleindorf's Meats—so suddenly that I think he's gotten an itching to run in and pick up a brisket or something, but no. He turns to me with his tight, white lips and says, "Ivy Green, there's no 'best conversation' to be had here, do you understand? Your mama has gone off after that godforsaken preacher. She's left us and her medication behind, and there's not a darn thing to do about it, at least for a guy who's got even a shred of pride left. Do you understand?"

The air in my lungs goes straight up into my throat. "No," I say. "I don't understand. I want to know what's going on! I want you to go find Mama and bring her home!"

And right then someone behind us beeps to remind us we're still at the stop sign, mucking up traffic, so Daddy starts up again and says very quietly—so quietly, I'm not sure I hear him right, "Sometimes you have to wait till a person wants to be found."

Each morning as I put up the cereal boxes or the peanut butter in the kitchen cupboard, I look at the pharmacy bag that Donnetta Snow sent home with us the other day. Daddy hasn't touched it since—it's just sitting there on the countertop, waiting for Mama to remember herself. Or remember us. Or something.

I tried one more time when we got home that day, suggesting maybe Daddy could send the pills to Mama if he wasn't going to go get her personally, and he said, "Ivygirl, I'm gonna be straight up with you: I do not know where to send them. Your mama didn't exactly leave behind a good address." And then he shut his eyes for a second—just a second, like an extra-long blink—and took a deep breath. It's hard to say if that was the scared dad or the mad dad, breathing like that, but either way, it didn't seem good.

I'd been hoping it was just me who didn't know how or where in heaven's name to find The Great Good Bible

Church of Panhandle Florida. (Well, except for being pretty sure that it's in Florida.) But it turns out that Daddy doesn't know either. Which I take to mean that Mama is actually missing. Or, like Daddy said, not wanting to be found.

"Let's go back to the jets!" says Devon as I'm putting him into the stroller. I've gotten so I can do this part myself so Mrs. Murray doesn't even have to come out with us in the morning.

"Your mama's right," I say to Devon. "You're a man with a plan." I start to strap him in, but he takes over and buckles himself. Which I guess is why we really don't need Mrs. Murray—it's not me getting more capable. It's Devon.

"See planes fly," says Lucy. She's like a little mockingbird now that she can talk, constantly copying Devon's words and ideas.

But really, her request is not a shock. Pretty much all that Devon and Lucy have wanted to do these last couple of weeks is watch remote control planes fly loop-the-loops in the airspace over East Loomer Park. It never seems to get boring—not for them, and not for me either. We don't know how they work. Or which way they're gonna turn next. Or how they can be up in the air, easy as birds, one moment, and thumping along the ground like a dog with a limp the next. But that's what we like, I think, all three of us. It's the surprise and mystery of it that makes us want to watch.

Meanwhile, it turns out that this is where Paul Dobbs usually hangs out too. Which means that I'm spending big chunks of almost every day with one of Loomer's official certified brainiac science guys.

I should clarify. We hang out, but we couldn't be considered real or actual friends, if being friends requires having something in common. Besides skipping out of church together, I mean.

My family couldn't be more different from Paul's if we tried. Mrs. Dobbs is a teller at the County Credit Union, and Paul's dad is the branch manager. Mrs. Dobbs is pretty if you like red hair, which I do—it is so much more interesting than all the other colors—and Mr. Dobbs is what Mama calls "distinguished." (Mama's always hoping Daddy will become a little more "distinguished," but Daddy says he's cleaned up as best he can.) Paul's sister, Jenny, is redheaded like their mama, and she's part of the popular group.

But Paul says he's about as different from the rest of

the Dobbses as I am. "They've never once come over to watch me fly," he told me one day. "It's not that they're mean about it—they even gave me a fancy new remote for my birthday this year—but they just don't get it."

I don't tell him that we don't really "get it" either, but that's okay by me. And Lucy. And Devon.

Paul isn't a redhead like his mama and sister, and he isn't exactly distinguished-looking either, but he *is* nice to look at. For a boy that I'm always getting a little mad at, I mean. This morning we're back on the topic of the space shuttle and how we aren't gonna know a thing about the universe anymore, once the space shuttle gets laid up for good.

"The only folks who're gonna be up there are robots and rich folks," Paul says. "'Cause that's the new thing, y'know. It's not even for scientists anymore. It's for tourists! If you've got enough money, you can fly. Otherwise, forget it."

"Well, good for the rich people," I say. "Honestly. Who cares? You and your friends are playing with fire, Paul Dobbs, thinking scientists have all the answers in the whole wide world. You're not paying a lick of attention or respect to God, who is the real answer man. I mean, you'd think the world was coming to an end instead of just a simple space program."

I look at Paul through the fence, his fingers hooked onto the metal loops like they're holding him up. My fingers rest on Devon's and Lucy's heads, like *they're* what's holding me up.

"Is that so? You're so sure about God?" Paul says, and he sounds a little angry. But I can see around his lips that he's almost laughing a little too.

And then he says, "Well, I think you and Abby and Kimmy and y'all are just silly. You're always swearing by these made-up fairy tales about a 'God' that nobody's ever even seen in person. It's one thing for grown-ups to buy the whole thing, but we're young! We should be more . . . skeptical!" Which was a Mrs. Murray vocab word, by the way. So he does listen in English after all. "At least I care about something actual, something testable," he says. "That's the kind of thing a person ought to believe in, if you ask me."

And then Paul unhooks his fingers and shrugs a little, like he doesn't want to be pushy about it. Even though he is being pretty pushy, if you ask me. I guess we both are, never mind that we're not really getting anywhere.

"So, hey," I ask, "do you want to share our crackers and our grapes?" 'Cause they're real and actual too, and I'm hungry. And the next thing you know, Paul Dobbs and I are sitting up on Picnic Hill with the Murray babies. Which becomes sort of our habit almost every afternoon in June.

I'm at home on an off day from the Murrays, trying to come up with something for Daddy and me to have for dinner, something hot and homemade that might fill up the very quiet space that's taken over our kitchen. Chicken Kiev, maybe. Or something with dumplings or a crust. And then there's a knock on our screen door. "Who is it?" I yell as I walk from the kitchen toward the knocking.

"It's Abby, silly." By now I can see her straight through the screen, so I guess that does make it kind of a silly question.

"Hey, Abby. What's up? Wanna come in? I'm making a PB and J." Because the truth is, while I've been dreaming about dinner, I've actually been half-making a sandwich and half-turning pages in Mama's cookbooks while I do.

I pull the door open, and the hinges squeak and cry. Abby floats in. Abby's what Mama calls "conventionally pretty," with her blond silky braids and white tank top and short striped skirt. She's tan but not at all burned, and her toenails are pink.

Mama calls her conventionally pretty to make me feel better when I complain about being not all that pretty or popular in school. "You're more unique," is how she put it once.

But Abby's pretty through and through, and I'm not all that unique. I'm actually a little mousy, with sort of light brown everything. But I didn't argue, 'cause if I did, Mama'd start in on how I'm beautiful inside and out, blah, blah, blah, having nothing to do with the truth and everything to do with me being her little girl.

"I can't stay, but thanks for asking. Mother says I need new shoes, which doesn't make any sense if you consider the fact that it's summer and I walk around barefoot all the time. But . . ." She trails off.

"But what?"

Abby's followed me into the kitchen, where I go back to my sandwich making, so I'm not looking at her when she says, "Oh, never mind. I shouldn't bring up going shopping with my mama when your mama's run off and all."

"My mama did not run off, Abby Newton." I pivot around and face her head-on. "I don't know where you got that idea. She's . . . studying. That's what. She's studying the Bible. Haven't you ever heard of The Great Good Bible Church of Panhandle Florida? Sheesh."

I realize too late that I am shaking a butter knife straight at her, and it's dripping with grape jelly that looks like the petrified blood from a cow's eye in science lab. I set the knife back down on the counter next to the open jelly jar and Mama's cookbooks.

"Sorry," I say.

"Gosh, me too," says Abby. "I was actually trying to be nice," she says.

It's always been true with Abby Newton that her "trying to be nice" doesn't necessarily look or feel nice. But I don't think that's all her fault. It's partly due to her voice, I think, which usually comes out about three squeaks too high.

Still, I feel bad for snapping at her and for threatening her with murder-by-butter-knife. "I know it. I know you were. I'm feeling a little sensitive," I say. "Sorry, Abby. You want a quick sandwich after all?"

"Sure," says Abby, and we're both quiet for a second.

I'm thinking that she's probably noticing the crumbs and the newspapers piling up and the other stuff in our kitchen, which just isn't right without Mama here. But it turns out that isn't what she's thinking at all.

"Hey, Ivy. You have a boyfriend you've been meaning to tell me about?" she asks as I slap her sandwich shut.

And I feel myself blush, probably purple as the jelly. I don't have a boyfriend, that's for sure, but I do know who she's talking about. And if Abby's talking about him, half of Loomer is too. They've probably got me near married to Paul Dobbs, science guy.

"I think the sun's getting to you," I say, and I cut her sandwich into triangles and slide it toward her on a paper towel. Then I bite into mine before she gets me saying another thing.

Chapter Six

The day the postcard arrives from Mama, I've been flopping around at the city pool all afternoon with Abby and Kimmy. It is blazing hot outside. And poor Daddy's been up on a roof, where it's even hotter than down here. We show up at home right at the same time.

"How can you stand working outside in this heat, Daddy?" I hold the door open for him as we walk inside, and I head straight to the thermostat to crank the A/C up to cold.

Daddy peels off his T-shirt, right there in the kitchen. He's so wet, he looks like he's been the one at the pool.

"You know what I always say, baby. I'm closer to the angels when I'm on a roof than when I'm on the ground. Even when it's a hundred and two." He pops open a cold soda and gulps most of it down without stopping for a breath.

"Will you grab the mail, Ivy?" Daddy says, finishing off his soda and wiping his mouth with his T-shirt. "I'm gonna hop in the shower, and then we'll get some dinner started. Deal?"

So of course he's already in the shower when I drop my butt straight down onto the porch hard, because I've got a postcard from Mama in my hands. On the front is the word "Mobile," all done up in purple cursive neon. I don't have a clue why she'd send us a card that says "Mobile," until I turn it over and see, in little printing, *Mobile, Alabama. Population 195,822 people, strong and proud.*

Oh! It's a town! I was thinking "mobile" as in "on the move."

Which would've made sense for Mama.

Beneath the information on Mobile, Alabama, there's Mama's familiar handwriting, in blue ink. It's curvy and round, nicer than mine, and sort of school-girly. Mama's writing is one of the things that marks her as young, for a mama, I mean. Younger than most of my friends' moms, at least, with her pretty skin and shiny hair and school-girly cursive. That's what happens when you have your baby straight out of high school, I suppose. You're still young, even when you're a mama.

"Oh, Mama," I say. I cannot help but say it out loud, sitting here on the hot wood planks of our porch with this tiny postcard in my hands. I am so distracted and heart-fluttery over her inked letters that it takes me a second to actually get to reading the words.

> *Dear Max and Ivy,*
>
> *As you can see, I got this in Alabama, on our drive. I guess a card from Alabama doesn't mean much if you've only driven through it. The Great Good Bible Church is something different than I expected. How are you? I'm running out of room. You know I love you.*

And then it isn't even signed because, sure enough, she ran out of room.

Here's the not-very-good thing about postcards: they don't leave a person an ounce of extra room for details, like "Here's where I am" and "Here's when I'll be back."

Daddy's still mopping off his hair with a towel when he walks back into the kitchen to make dinner, and I'm sitting at the table, all dizzyish, like I've seen a ghost.

"I'm thinking pasta, huh, Ives?" he says, before he notices the card on the table in front of me, my hands on either side of it, shaking. I've read it probably twenty times by now, and it still hasn't told me a thing.

"What's that you've got, baby?" Daddy reaches for the card, and I hear his breath suck in as he sees Mama's handwriting. Then there's dead silence while he reads.

When he finally says something, it's this: "Well, I pray God is looking after her." That's it. That's what he says. He doesn't stop to wonder where she is, or how she's getting by without her medications, or what she means that The Great Good Bible Church is different than she expected.

"You're praying? Daddy, explain to me why you are praying," I say. "What can God do about any of this? Aren't you the least bit mad at God? We wouldn't be in this fix in the first place if it weren't for God."

Daddy's mouth actually falls open, and I have to admit I'm surprising myself too, but what's a prayer gonna do for us right now? "We've gone to church all our livelong days," I say, "and put our collection money in the basket, and volunteered in the food pantry, and still here we are, Mama run off to Florida without her pills, us left behind to worry, and nothing but a postcard in more than a month! Do you think that's truly and indeed the best that God can do?"

"Ivy. You stop right this second," says Daddy, his mouth back under his control. He drops the towel and the postcard and slams his hands on the tabletop. "You—"

But I don't let him finish. Words come out of me, hard and fast, like a drum beating. I can't help it.

"If I were you," I shout, "I'd be mad at God and mad at Mama, too! She ran off, Daddy—at least that's what people are saying. Do you know that, that people think Mama ran off? Is it true? Did Mama run off with Hallelujah Dave?" And right as I say it, I get the meaning I'd been missing all along. Maybe Mama really, truly did run off, y'know, *with* Hallelujah Dave. Like, not as a preacher so much as a boyfriend.

I swallow to keep my heart from coming up through my throat.

Daddy doesn't say a word at first. And then his voice is low and quaky—really quaky—like we're driving on a gravel road instead of sitting at the kitchen table. "Don't let's make things worse than they are by saying things about God you'll regret later on, Ivy Green. We need God, you and me, now more than ever, and I think we'd be wise not to take our anger out on the wrong guy." Which I take to mean that Daddy *is* mad at someone, whether he's saying so or not.

Also? He doesn't tell me I'm wrong about Mama, not at all. He just pulls out a chair and sits down heavily, right next to me, close enough that I can still feel the quaking.

"Daddy?" I say, kind of sorry-like. 'Cause I'm starting to think maybe *he's* the wrong guy to be mad at too, if you know what I mean.

"Ivy, your mama saw those piney woods burn down to the ground, and her daddy's church burnt right along with them, and it about broke her heart. Most people would've lost faith, but not Diana. She was not gonna stop praying just 'cause God is hard to understand. She just set out to pray harder. I've got to believe that's what she's doing now, and I've got to believe that's what we should be doing too."

Daddy picks the postcard back up and holds it between his two hands like it's an extra hand—like it's *Mama's* hand—as if he's gonna put Mama herself right smack in the middle of his prayer. He looks so sad, I just don't have the heart to fight him any further, so I hop up to fill a pot with water.

"Okay, Daddy. Okay," I say. "We're tired and hungry, right? So, what about that pasta? Should we go for the fancy kind since we heard from Mama? To sort of . . . celebrate?"

"Celebratory pasta." Daddy laughs a tired but not-mad Daddy laugh and lets the card drop out of his hands onto the table. "You are my kinda girl, Ivy Green. My kinda girl."

So we cook the fancy pasta, which just means ordinary old noodles but with butter and canned clams on top, and we talk about everything except for Mama as we eat. It's a nice night. But in the back of my head, quiet as a mouse, is a little voice that says, *Daddy may not be mad at God, but I am. And I'm pretty sure I'm mad at Mama, too.*

Chapter Seven

Some days are plain unlucky. Like today. I get a flat tire on my way to the Murrays' and have to push my bike the rest of the way. Then it turns out Lucy has a summer cold with a runny nose, and she fusses the whole way to the park, and I get green snot on my pretty yellow shirt when I bend down to love her up. And Devon somehow loses a shoe between there and here.

Plus the day started with Mama's postcard sitting out on the kitchen counter again. It keeps popping up and reminding me that Daddy's been worrying, which makes me double worry—about Mama and about him, too.

And now here we are to watch the flying machines— which is what I'd promised Lucy and Devon the whole snotty, shoe-losing nine blocks to the park—and it's closed. Empty. Shut down, with a sign on the gate saying, NO MOTORIZED AIRCRAFT UNTIL FURTHER NOTICE BY ORDER OF THE CITY OF LOOMER.

"Well, huh, guys," I say. "There's nobody flying today."

Devon starts to cry. Lucy sneezes. I wipe sweat and

sunscreen away from my eyes, drop the backpack onto the ground next to the stroller, and flop down beside it. If I were a tire, *I'd* be flat.

"I thought you guys might be here." Paul Dobbs kind of jogs toward us from Picnic Hill, looking over his shoulder a couple of times. His voice sounds funny, as if he's got a cold too, like Lucy. And he's wearing a hoodie over his T-shirt, even though it's ninety-something degrees outside.

"Well, yeah. We're here, but what happened? Why is the airspace closed down? Mr. Devon Murray is none too pleased," I say, "so neither am I."

Devon hushes his crying a little bit 'cause Paul's here, and Devon just plain likes Paul. Lucy likes him too, and I can see why. Paul's funny with them. He makes goofy voices, and he rolls down Picnic Hill like a barrel, and he knows how to make model airplanes fly like magic. What's not to like, really?

"Ha. Welcome to my world," says Paul, not sounding nice or funny or goofy at all. "It's like my own mini version of the space shuttle program shutting down. Some jerk complained about the noise coming from the airspace, and then they decide that maybe it's too dangerous anyway—noisy *and* dangerous. And that's it. No more flying. Just like that."

Paul plops down onto the grass next to us and pulls Devon onto his lap. "I'm never gonna get the chance to be a real astronaut, and now I don't even get to pretend anymore. Plus a freaking dog chased me half the way here, but I guess the City of Loomer doesn't care about that kind of noisy and dangerous, does it?" And he looks around, like the dog might still be coming.

"My summer's just junk," he says. "The Space-Junk Summer of Doom," he says, kind of kicking the ground in front of him as he talks.

Which makes me hop up and kind of kick my feet at him!

"*Your* summer is junk? *Your* summer? Seriously, Paul Dobbs, you should think of somebody other than yourself for one hot minute. I don't think your bike tire's flat, you don't have green snot all down your shirt, and I'm 100 percent certain that your mama's not gone missing!" I am half-shouting by the time I finish, and also half-hoarse 'cause I've got a lump in my throat again. (I don't even mention that it hurts my feelings when he says his summer's been junk, when he's spent a whole lot of it with me.)

"Ivy sad?" Lucy stands up and puts one hand on each of my hips.

"Wait, what? Your mom is really missing?" Paul asks, and he stands up too. "I thought she was at church camp or something. I didn't know she was missing, Ivy. Honest."

And now I start to cry, for real. For the first time since Mama left forty-six days ago, I cry and cry and cry. There is something about both Lucy and Paul being soft and nice to me that makes everything feel even sadder, and two heavy streams of tears wash down my face. When I look up at Paul and then out across the park, at the hill and the playgrounds and the little kid learning to ride his bike, it all blurs and stings, and even though I want to, I don't quite know how to stop.

So I talk straight through the tears. "Well, she's not missing exactly, but we don't have the foggiest idea where she is." And then I cry some more.

"Ivy have mom?" asks Lucy.

"Ivy does have a mom," says Paul, "and we should go find her."

That's really what he says. "We should go find her."

Which makes my tears just up and stop, pretty suddenly. I look back at Paul and see him, truly, clear as day.

We should go find Mama? I've been waiting for Daddy to go find her, ever since she left, but me? Me and Paul? That's something that never, not even once, occurred to me. So much for me being an idea girl.

I wipe my eyes, swallow the feeling-sorry-for-myself stuff, and say, "Um, what? Paul? Seriously?"

"Yeah," he says. "Seriously." And then he smiles.

I agree to meet Paul at the church steps in a couple of hours, on my way home from the Murrays'. Which is kind of embarrassing, because once you set a time and a place, it could technically be considered a date. I figure someone will see us and the word will spread, and we all know what Abby's gonna have to say about that.

There's no such thing as a secret in Loomer. Pastor Lou even put that on the marquee outside of church once, and then he gave a sermon about it, about how we're all naked in God's eyes.

"Amen, brother," everyone said. "Aaa-men." Like it was a good thing. But as I roll into the parking lot of Second Baptist on my bike, I think, *Why on earth would we all be okay with God seeing us naked?* Especially when Pastor Lou also preaches that we're supposed to be modest and everything.

I swear, religion makes less sense every day. It's no wonder Mama's taken to acting so funny, when you think of all the messages she's gotten over the years, from Pastor Lou and Hallelujah Dave and her very own daddy. She's spent her whole life long listening to bossy, confusing religious folks tell her what to do.

I lock my bike to the side fence and walk past the marquee on my way to find Paul. Today it reads, THE ONLY BUSINESS WE OUGHT TO PAY ATTENTION TO IS OUR OWN.

Which I take to mean that maybe some secrets aren't so bad after all.

Paul actually looks better than he looked a while ago at the park, like his cold just cleared right up. And don't take my word for it, because it's a matter of opinion, I'm sure, but there is something kind of cute about Paul Dobbs. Or maybe I've just been seeing so much of him, he's grown on me. But whatever. Here's the thing:

He doesn't look like a science guy or a jock or a Godhead or a skater. He doesn't wear glasses. His hair isn't supershort, but it isn't really long either. He's not all muscley or superscrawny, and his T-shirts don't say anything to give him away. He's just Paul, which either makes him sort of plain or makes him a genuine mystery—I'm not sure which. But I kind of like it.

And, this is interesting. His hair is the exact color of mine, but I wouldn't call his mousy, even though that's always what I've called mine. It's prettier than mousy, if you can call a boy's hair pretty—more like caramel, which makes me hate my own hair less.

Mama would say, "My mercy, Ivy Green, you fixate on the littlest things when we've got God's great big world to pay attention to. Head out of the clouds, little missy. Head out of the clouds." (Even though Mama fixates on her own hair sometimes. She truly does.)

Anyway, here's kind-of-cute Paul Dobbs, a little twitch in his smile, sitting on the cellar steps, just the way I found him when I skipped out of service a few weeks back.

"Oh, hey, Ivy," says Paul, standing up. "You came. Good. Okay, well, here's the deal. We can take a Greyhound bus to Florida and be there in a day. Eighteen hours, to be exact, if we go from, like, Houston to Tallahassee. And let's face it, it's gonna be easier to find your mom's church once we're actually there in Florida, right? People are gonna have heard of it. So if we leave, like, maybe tomorrow . . ."

Paul is waving a spiral notebook as he talks. He's got bus schedules and the names of towns written down, and it suddenly occurs to me that he might be 100 percent totally serious, not kidding at all about this whole thing.

"Whoa, whoa! Hang on, Paul." My voice shakes a little, and I don't know if it's 'cause I'm excited or 'cause I'm scared. What in heaven's name would Mama or Daddy or the good Lord have to say about *this* idea?

"Seriously," I say. "Hang on a minute. I have a lot of questions."

"Good. Questions are good," says Paul. "They're my specialty." And he laughs as if this whole thing is a joke, only it isn't.

"Paul Dobbs," I say, "you better hope that *answers* are your specialty, if you think I'm getting on a Greyhound bus and going anywhere with you. I don't care whose mama we're looking for."

Paul's face falls, and his eyes are instantly a little less shiny. I actually feel kind of bad for snapping at him, because it looks like I've hurt his feelings and I'm pretty sure he's only trying to help.

"Sorry," I say. "That was rude of me. But this is all a little crazy, you have to admit." I slide onto the steps next to Paul, and we both sit down.

"Yeah, it's crazy. But in a good way. Look, you've got to have a bunch of babysitting money, don't you? And I'm gonna sell some of my planes and stuff. I've already figured that out. So we should be good for the bus tickets," says Paul.

"Your planes? You're going to sell your planes?" I can't believe it. "You love your planes!" It's then I notice the big tote bag leaning against the railing behind Paul, full to bursting with flying machines. He really *is* 100 percent serious, not at all kidding, isn't he?

And I don't know if I should be glad about that or not. I may be full of ideas, but that's about it. I don't *do* the things I dream up. I go to school. I babysit. I ask Mama and Daddy for a dog, over and over and over again. I don't aim to be an astronaut or an airplane pilot or anything wild at all, and I surely don't intend to be a runaway.

"Y'know what? I did love 'em, but they're just toys," says Paul. I start to interrupt, but he stops me. "And, Ivy, you don't have to pretend that they're not, just to make me feel better. Plus, the airspace is closed. And it's not like I can pretend like I'm working toward something real, with the shuttle program shutting down. It's time to kiss space good-bye and start thinking about something more realistic, like being a doctor or something. My dad's been telling me that since the day I was born anyway, so, big surprise. He's right."

Paul doesn't sound like a guy who thinks his dad is right. He sounds like a guy who's sad. But I can't think of a single thing that might fix that.

"Sorry," I say, kind of softly, but I know that's not enough.

"C'mon," he says. "Let's make a plan."

Like it's been decided.

So we do. We sit on the steps of Second Baptist that are so hot, they almost burn the backs of my legs, and we open up Paul's notebook, and we start to figure things out, like how much money we need and what we'll tell our parents and what we'll do when we arrive in the panhandle of Florida. (*If* we arrive in the panhandle of Florida.)

I tell Paul that's another not-good thing about The Great Good Bible Church of Panhandle Florida: "It should be called The Great Good Bible Church of THE Panhandle OF Florida. Shouldn't it? It's THE Panhandle! That's the sort of mistake that would drive Mrs. Murray half-crazy—"

And then I interrupt myself. "Oh, gosh. Wait a minute," I say. "What about the Murrays? Mrs. Murray's expecting me, every day but Tuesdays. She needs me, and I'll be letting her down if I'm suddenly not there."

"Now, that's kind of funny," says Paul.

"What?"

"That you're more worried about Mrs. Murray than you are about your own dad."

And Paul's right. I'm not really thinking too much about Daddy, because if I think about Daddy, I think about getting caught—as a runaway, for goodness' sake—and that gives me the chill-bumps. Plus, it doesn't seem to me that Daddy (or God, for that matter) has done such a great job of looking after Mama lately, which is why it's been left completely up to me. Well, me and Science Boy here, if that's not the strangest thing.

"Okay, fine," I say. "Mrs. Murray will be fine. She's resourceful." Which was another one of our vocab words this year, by the way. Plus, she is. "Now, here's what I think, Paul Dobbs . . ."

And this idea comes out of my mouth before it's even really solid in my head. "If we're going all the way to Florida," I say, "I think we better go see the space shuttle too. I mean, that's where they keep it, right? Or where they keep *them*, since there are a few of them, like you told me? If you're gonna kiss space good-bye after all these years of loving it so much you wanted to marry it, then it seems like you oughta break up in person. Right?"

I turn to look at Paul, sitting so close to me that we're practically stuck together. I want to see what he thinks of my half-cocked idea. And wow. I promise you that right that very minute? His eyes start to shine again. Like stars.

Chapter Eight

Before leaving for the Murrays' in the morning, I pack my school backpack with a few pairs of underwear; my toothbrush, hairbrush, and some hairbands; two hundred and sixty dollars in babysitting money; and a box of granola bars Daddy brought home with the shopping yesterday.

When we said good-bye outside the church last night, Paul told me to be ready to go at a moment's notice, "So that as soon as I get the money I need, we can take off."

I was about to tell him to stop being pushy, but then I thought I probably wouldn't step one foot outside of Loomer, Texas, without Paul being a little pushy, so I said okay. And here I am, packing. I shiver when I zip up my bag, and my brain says, *No, no!* but then I interrupt myself and think, *Yes.*

I look around my room to distract myself—the room Mama let me decorate in third grade—and lordamercy, I have grown so deathly ill of this pink. It's like bubble gum stuck in Hello Kitty's fur, and when I get back home with Mama, I'm gonna ask if we can do something about it.

"When I get back home," is what I said to myself, which means it's not just Paul who's 100 percent serious anymore. Who cares if the farthest I've ever been is Galveston? I'm going to find my mama in Florida. I just am. Yes, yes, no matter what, yes.

I run downstairs into the kitchen and grab Mama's medicines off the counter. And there, behind the bag, quietly plugged in next to the toaster, is her phone. When she first left, we thought she'd taken it with her. I called her every day, partly just to hear her voice on the voice mail but also so that she'd hear mine. Then Daddy found the phone sitting in her makeup drawer in the bathroom.

"Doesn't have her phone, hasn't used her credit card, and must not care that we don't know where in the world she's gone," said Daddy when he brought the phone downstairs and tossed it on the counter.

I looked at it after he'd left the room. There were a whole bunch of messages on it, and the battery was nearly dead. I stopped calling, and it's been here waiting on the counter, plugged in, ever since.

I don't know if it'd officially be considered stealing to take it, but it seems like a good idea either way. Mama shouldn't have gone all the way to Florida without a phone, and neither should we.

I don't have a phone of my own. Daddy says that Loomer's so small, you can just holler if you need something. Which isn't true, but I'm too busy trying to talk him into a dog, which I want more than a phone, and I can only fight so many battles at one time.

So Mama's phone will do. I grab it, shut it down to save power, and grab the charger out of the wall too. Then I notice the coffee cup in the sink. Daddy left early to put on a new roof—on another one of the houses damaged by the wildfires. "I'd never be grateful for someone's misfortune," he always says when he heads off for these jobs, "but I'm grateful for good work." And the fires made a whole lot of good work. That's just the truth. (It's also ironic, seeing as how they're the same fires that drove Mama half-crazy and all the way to Florida, but he never mentions that.)

Anyway, here I am packing to run away, with Daddy off at work and his coffee cup sitting in the sink like it's a totally ordinary normal old day. He has no idea. It's enough to give me the shivers again.

"Ivy, honey," says Mrs. Murray as we're putting together today's snacks, "I am going to work at the library today, so you and Lucy and Devon can stay and play here for a change. It'll help me focus, and you all maybe could use a day of being a little lazy. Is that all right?"

"Sure, we'll play here. It'll be fun. Won't it be fun, little bugs?" I pull Lucy up onto my hip and kiss her fat, happy cheek just a tidge longer than usual, since I know I'm gonna miss her when I'm gone. Mrs. Murray keeps cutting up fruit while Lucy and I watch.

"You do such a good job with them, Ivy. You are a natural. You know how to tend to them. I didn't know what to do with babies when I first had mine, but with you it just seems to be in your blood."

Which is kind of a funny thing to say to a girl whose own mother is off rolling around on the floor of a church in Florida instead of taking care of her family here at home. But still, it's nice, and it makes me feel bad again about leaving them with no warning at all.

"I don't think I'm that good at it, really," I say. "I mean, I'm only with them for a few hours, and you're their mom. You're with them all the time. That's a whole lot. I mean, I can't imagine how you know when you're ready to do that kind of thing. Y'know, get married and have babies and everything?"

"Mommy, peanut butter!" Lucy reaches toward Mrs. Murray, who takes her from my arms and pops a little square of peanut butter toast right into her mouth. Then she breathes a deep breath and turns back to me.

"Well, *that* is a mystery," says Mrs. Murray. "You never really know, sweet girl. There is so, so much in this world—both good and bad—that you never really know. You just have to learn to listen to that voice inside, the voice in you that is your own best self, to figure out what to do and when to do it."

She sets Lucy down and spreads more toast.

I can't help but think that if Mama'd listened to the voice inside instead of the voice that was Hallelujah Dave's, I wouldn't be fixing to skip out on Mrs. Murray and her babies like I am.

"And the rest of the time," she says, in one of her rushy-talky streams, "you have to learn to live with the mystery. There's not a way around that, no matter how old you are."

"My problem is, I've got a lot of voices inside," I say. "They interrupt one another all the time."

Mrs. Murray laughs. "Oh, Ivy. You're a lot like me. That's what breathing's for. And meditating, or praying. To calm down those voices and see if you can hear a single one, clear as a bell."

Maybe poor Mama has the same problem I have with

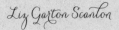

hearing a single voice. Although, you'd think with all of her praying, she'd have found it by now.

"Bells make music," says Devon, and he starts banging on the cabinets and stomping his feet in a little dance. Mrs. Murray laughs again.

I'm pushing Devon in the swing chair when Lucy runs down the hallway into her mama and daddy's bedroom. I don't know why it feels a little harder to keep track of the babies here at home than it does at the park. Maybe because I don't have remote control flying machines to keep them entertained. Maybe because I keep thinking of my packed backpack waiting in my room at home. Maybe because I keep thinking of Paul.

I'm realizing that I'm sad about the airspace closing, and about Paul selling his planes—not just for him but for me and for the Murray babies too. We got to love the whole thing nearly as much as he did, I think. And now here we are stuck at home, indoors, with blocks and puzzles and the swing chair, and we're all a little out of sorts.

"Stay swinging," I say to Devon, and I follow Lucy, even though it feels kind of private to march into Mr. and Mrs. Murray's room. Lucy toddles through the bedroom into the closet, and when I catch up with her, she is next to the dirty clothes hamper and a big jumbled box of shoes.

"Whatcha doing, Luce?" I ask.

Lucy turns around, and I see behind her a little night-stand with a tall purple candle in the middle, and some smooth stones, and a fat pretty pinecone standing on end. And there are three tiny pictures in frames—blurry old-fashioned black-and-white ones—and a silver baby rattle and a statue of Buddha. I mean, I think it's Buddha because it doesn't look like Gandhi, and I don't think they make statues of Gandhi anyway.

I wish I could ask Mrs. Murray about all this, but I shouldn't have let Lucy make it all the way down the hall away from me in the first place, and I shouldn't be snooping around in the Murrays' bedroom closet either. But suddenly and more than anything, I want to know what you're supposed to do with a little nightstand and a purple candle and a statue of Buddha. Is there something holy or magic here that might help me find my mama, or even help me know if what I'm about to do is right or wrong? I stand stock-still for a second and stare at the pretty little altar, waiting.

"Ivy," says Lucy, and she pulls on my fingers, away from what I'm trying to understand.

"Right. C'mon, Lucy. Let's go." I swoop her up and turn around, and back we go to Devon, who is yelling from the swing, "Down, Ivy. Down, down, right this minute down!"

And as I listen to him with one ear and Lucy with the other, I think about Mrs. Murray and the voices in *her* head, and I wonder if that's one of the great-good things about Buddha. Maybe he helps a person hear things, clear as a bell.

The home phone rings and rings as I unlock the back door of our house. I run inside and reach across the kitchen counter to catch it before it goes to voice mail. These days neither Daddy or I is willing to risk letting a phone ring without answering it, because one of these times it's just sure to be Mama.

"Hello?" I'm out of breath.

"Ivy? What's the matter? You sound funny." Kimmy is like Abby in that even when she's being nice, she doesn't necessarily sound nice. I guess that's one of the reasons they're perfect friends for each other. They can be not-very-nice-seeming together and then tell each other not to worry about it.

"I just got home," I say. "I rode my bike clear across

town and I'm out of breath. What's up, Kimmy?"

I hold the phone to my ear with my shoulder and pull open the refrigerator, hoping it'll look better than it does. It looks like *everyone* living here is out of town for the summer, not just Mama.

"Wanna go to the pool?" asks Kimmy. "A bunch of us are going. You can ride your bike, or Abby's mom will drive. Either way. Should we pick you up?"

Which I guess is Kimmy's way of deciding that I *am* going, since she didn't exactly wait for me to say yes or no. Which, I have to admit, makes me kind of glad. I tell her I'll ride my bike and I'll be there in a half hour.

The instant we hang up, the phone rings again. I can see from the caller ID that it's just another Loomer number, but still. Daddy says Hallelujah Dave could have a local number, for all we know. We can't be too sure.

But when I pick it up, it's not Mama or Hallelujah Dave. It's Paul.

"You ready?"

My heart starts to thump really hard, in a scary kind of way, like it might pound through the skin in my chest.

Ready?

Does he mean now?

"Do you mean now?" I ask out loud. Would I ever be

actually and truly ready to leave a note for Daddy and jump on a bus and go looking for my mama at a church that doesn't have a website or address or proper name or anything?

"Well, not *right* now," he says. "Not tonight, but what about first thing tomorrow morning? We could take the early bus to Houston and go from there?"

"Yeah, I guess I am," I say, because my backpack's packed and I've got money and a telephone, and at least Paul Dobbs is coming with me.

I pull the peanut butter off the shelf and dip a spoon deep into the jar. I don't think I'm really hungry, but I sure am nervous.

"But I mean, are *you* ready?" I ask. "Are we really gonna do this? Is this crazy? Is this safe? Did you sell your planes? Are you scared? Are you sure?" I stop myself from asking a hundred other questions, by popping the peanut butter into my mouth. It's sticky and sweet.

"Well, yeah," says Paul. "I think I'm ready. And I think it's crazy, too, but a lot of great ideas are at least a little bit crazy. Don't you think?"

I don't answer, because I don't *know* the answer to that. I guess he's talking about taking a leap of faith, right? Except for the fact that Paul Dobbs probably wouldn't put it that way, due to the word "faith" and all.

"Y'know who wanted all my flying gear? Dash. He's always wanted a bigger collection, and he obviously gets some kind of whopping allowance, because he bought everything. Perfect, huh?"

"Yep. Wow. Perfect. You didn't tell him, though, did you? This has to be top secret, right?" My voice comes out funny 'cause of all the peanut butter, but I'm serious. If a single soul knows about this, we won't make it to see the space shuttle in Cape Canaveral or The Great Good Bible Church in Tallahassee or even, probably, the bus station in Houston.

"Top secret," says Paul. And I believe him, because for whatever reason, he seems to want to make it to Florida at least as much as I do.

aul and I'd agreed to meet at the end of my street at ten till six in the morning with everything we'd need. So at five twenty my alarm shakes me awake. Last night I stowed it under my pillow so it wouldn't disturb Daddy, which you have to admit was a good idea, but it is startling, like my own head is a fire alarm, clanging.

I turn it off and roll over onto my back and stare at the ceiling of my own little room in Loomer, Texas. I think about lying to Daddy and to Mrs. Murray, and about getting onto a bus with Paul Dobbs, of all the people on God's green earth. I think about going all the way to Florida and maybe—or maybe not—finding Mama, and then I stop, because I simply cannot think about not finding Mama.

I tiptoe into the bathroom, pee without flushing, and brush my teeth without water. I can't make a single mistake, or the whole thing is off.

For the first time in my life, I'm glad that I don't have a dog. A dog would hear me and bark, or come panting after me down the stairs and wake Daddy. So it's good

I'm all alone, tiptoeing around this quiet house. When I get back from Florida, though, I'm gonna go right back to wanting a dog. I just want to get that on the record.

It's five forty when I set the note I pre-wrote on the kitchen table and sneak out the door toward the garage. By seven, I'll be on a bus to Houston, and Daddy will be drinking his coffee, surprised that I forgot to tell him about having to babysit extra early for the Murrays today.

That's not like Ivy, he'll think. *That's not like Ivy at all.*

And it's true, it's not. But hopping a Greyhound bus to Florida isn't either, and I'm doing that, so I guess some days are just full of surprises.

It's still that creepy kind of dark outside, and the street-light near the front of our house sizzles like a bug zapper as I ride beneath it. My blood beats hard, not only in my chest but in my head and hands too, and I'm not sure if that's just because I'm riding fast or because I'm scared of getting caught or because I'm afraid that if I don't get caught, I'm really, truly, honest to goodness going to do this. I'm going to run away.

Paul says we're not running away. He says we're going on an exploratory field trip, but somehow I'm thinking that Daddy isn't going to see it that way. To be honest, I'm not 100 percent sure *what* Daddy is going to think about this whole thing. He's been not really all that Daddyish ever since Mama left, and I don't blame him for that, but I can't just sit here in Loomer and wait for him to come around.

I see the silhouette of Paul and his bike standing under another buzzing streetlight a few blocks down, at the corner of Magpie and Lowey. His backpack hangs off one shoulder, and one of his feet is still up on a bike pedal, as if he might take off at any moment. I roll quietly nearer and nearer to him until I can actually see his face, yellow in the light.

"Why are you standing under the light for all the world to see?" My voice comes out louder than I expected, a sort of yelled whisper.

"Why are you yelling for all the world to hear?" Paul yell-whispers back. I guess we're both a little tense.

"Sorry," we say at once, and then, without another word, we turn our bikes out onto Lowey and head for the bus station. My pumping matches Paul's pumping, my breathing matches Paul's breathing, and the yellow-pink beginnings of the day shine at the end of the street like something sweet—a berry or a flower or a promise.

We lock our bikes around the corner from the station, near the Lazy Laundry, just like we planned. Because nobody'd look for us there, that's the sure truth. Inside the station almost all the seats are empty, except for three—an older man and woman who remind me of my Papa and Meemaw, Daddy's parents, which makes me sad because they've both passed on; and a man on his own, who I'm pretty sure is homeless. I recognize him from when our Bible study gave out clean socks and granola bars to people who were down on their luck, which, from the looks of it, he still is. So he makes me sad too, and I start to wonder if it's just a sad sort of morning. Or if maybe every morning's a little sad at the bus station.

"One way to Houston," says Paul to the girl in the booth. Because here's our plan:

1. We will buy one-way tickets because we're not exactly sure when we're coming back, or how, or who will be with us. (Please, Mama, be with us.)
2. We will buy tickets just to Houston, so that if anyone tracks us to the station, we won't have given away our final destination.

3. And we will buy tickets separately so that maybe the ticket girl won't know we're together. And that's an easy way to keep our money straight.

4. Also? You have to be fifteen to ride on the Greyhound alone—Paul found that out in his research—and since we are not exactly fifteen we plan to look as old as possible at all times. People like Mrs. Murray have always called me "mature," so that's what I'm counting on. Neither of us is wearing a school T-shirt at least, so that's a start.

Paul buys his one-way ticket to Houston, and I buy a bottle of Dr Pepper. And then, a few minutes later, after Paul's gone to the men's room and the homeless man has tipped over sideways in his seat, I step up to the window.

"A ticket to Houston, one way, please," I say, and I slide a little of my babysitting money across the counter. The girl, who has long, curved, tiger-print fingernails, slides a ticket back. She never even looks up.

"Here I come, Mama," I whisper as I walk away from the counter. "Everything is going to be okay. I promise you that. Everything is going to be okay."

And as the morning sun comes beating through the windows of the little station, I believe this, through and through.

Chapter Ten

We sit quietly in our seats as the bus starts up, hoping not to be noticed. Just like that, so quietly, and away we go. Right after we pass the big, beat-up sign for the county dump, the long lines of sooty, blackened trees appear. There was a week or so, not too long after the fires, when Daddy was coming out here all the time to help assess the damage and make bids on rebuilding the roofs. He said you could smell the smoke straight through the windows of his truck, and when he got home, his clothes smelled like he'd been camping. Now I lean into the rounded window at my shoulder and breathe in, but it just smells like bus.

Before long the skeleton trees are gone. Loomer is gone. *We* are really and truly gone. I'm sure we've got a long way to go before landing in Florida, but it feels like the hardest part of the trip is over already. We did it. We left.

I take another deep breath—more like a sigh this time—and I feel Paul do the same thing in the seat next to me.

"Y'know," I say. "I've spent nearly my whole long life wishing for a dog and wishing for a middle name."

"I'm not one for dogs," says Paul. And then a second or two later he says, "You don't have a middle name?"

"Ivy Blank Green," I say. "That's me."

"Well, what kind of a name is that?" asks Paul.

"A lame one," I say. "Mama and Daddy decided to skip the middle-name thing, like we always skip a verse when we're singing hymns at church? It was supposed to be meaningful—they were leaving room for God, they said—but to me it's just always felt like I was missing a name. And missing a dog. And now I'm missing a mama."

I sigh again, for real this time.

"Yeah," says Paul. "Yeah. Sorry."

I don't know what to do with myself after that. I wish I would've brought a book or something, because I have a feeling this is gonna be a really long ride. My fingers find the little cross I wear on a chain around my neck. It was Mama's when she was a girl, and it's been mine since Daddy got her a new one. I love it, even though the gold has worn off in places and you can see a sort of unshiny silver underneath. Which I guess means it's fake, but that doesn't really matter much to me.

I've pressed myself up against the corner of my seat to sleep for a little bit, on account of getting up early and all, when our bus hits something big. You can tell because there's a bounce and a terrible bang—I lurch awake—and the next thing you know, we're thumping off to the side of the road. Everyone around us sits up high and leans out into the aisle to see what's going on.

Our driver, an older woman who's so large, she uses the steering wheel like a handle to pull herself up, moves a lever to open the door with a big swooshing sound, and out she goes.

"Oh my God. This was a crappy idea," says Paul, too loud and kind of out of the blue. "The whole idea of leaving early was to get out of town—as far out of town as we could, before anyone realized we were gone. And now we're stuck on the side of the road? I knew it. This whole thing was really, really a crappy idea."

He sits to the right of me—trapping me up against the window—and he suddenly seems bigger than before, with a voice that's deep and mad. Even still, his hands shake and jitter on his knees.

I turn my body toward him, my back up against the side of the bus. "Hey!" I say. "What on God's green earth? This was your idea, Mr. Smart Man. And you're giving up on it, just like that? I ran away from home because of you, and you're giving up?"

I'm shaking too, my hands and my voice. What is happening here? We just left! We planned this all the way out, pretty carefully, and still, everything is falling apart before we've even made it to our first stop!

Our driver heaves herself back up the steps of the bus and booms, "Well, folks, as luck would have it, that was some heavy chunk of lumber we hit, and I believe our axle's broke, and we're gonna have to wait here for the mechanic to come and fix us up. Y'all make yourselves comfortable." And then she turns and plops back in her seat as if she doesn't have a place in the world to be.

I sink down low and wrap my arms around my body, tight. It's like I want to hold myself together so I don't start to cry.

"You're right," I whisper to Paul after a solid minute of just sitting and squeezing and not crying. "This was really, truly a bad idea."

I turn back to the window, rest my head against the frame, and look out at a tangled field of soybeans that goes on and on and on.

"Oh, dear God," I say, in that sort of yell-whisper I've used all morning. "Oh, please, please, please, dear God."

'Cause really, a little bit of God would come in handy right about now.

Everyone on the entire bus has to stand on the side of the road while the tow truck guy uses some fancy jack to raise the bus up toward the back of the truck.

"Wow. Would you look at that?" I say. "That is quite the tool. Daddy needs one of those to get himself up onto roofs. He could kiss his ladders good-bye!"

"It's a hydraulic lift," Paul says. What he's really saying is, "It's a hydraulic lift, you dummy." I can tell by the shake of his head and the sort of tone he takes.

Any fool who's been raised right would tell you I was just trying to be nice, to make conversation. But Paul has to do his it's-a-hydraulic-lift-you-dummy thing, and then he finishes with "Shhh."

"Shhh," as in to hush me!

Okay. I'm sorry, Mr. Boss of the World, but I don't think that being really quiet standing next to a gigantic Greyhound bus on the side of the road is gonna keep us from getting caught. And I don't think that being in a fight is gonna get us to Florida. (I mean, of course I don't actually say that, because I'm supposed to be quiet.)

Most other folks aren't quiet, by the way, because

they aren't running away from home and Paul Dobbs isn't their running-away partner. In fact, everyone else seems to think this is a little bit fun and worth making friends over, never mind that we're all standing in wobbly gravel and the tow truck's noisy and the sun is already hot.

The lady and man who were sitting a couple rows up from us, across the aisle from each other, seem to be discovering that they actually know each other from way back when. "It's a small world," the lady keeps saying.

"A mighty small world," the man answers.

Which makes me think of Mama, who, heaven knows, would not only be making friends with everyone on the bus but would also be giving them recipes and possibly starting a sing-along. She's polite and friendly that way, ten times more polite than I am. She'd be driving Paul Dobbs half-crazy if she were here right now.

"Blest be the tie that binds," I whisper under my breath, because Paul cannot keep me away from Mama's favorite hymn. He just plain can't.

"We pour our ardent prayers . . ." I whisper and I keep on going, all the way till the bit that says, "When we asunder part, it gives us inward pain," and I think, *that* is the real truth. I am parted from my mama, and I am inward pained. I am! And I don't understand why she isn't too! Why isn't *she* on a bus, coming for me? Whatever happened to the "family" part of my mama's moral fiber?

"Hey," says Paul all of a sudden. "Hey, now! A new bus! Lookit, Ivy. We're not even gonna have to get hauled back into town. We can leave from here!"

And he's right. A new bus—a perfect twin to the one we were on, only this one has all its pieces working right—pulls off into the gravel in front of ours. Our driver, the very gigantic (but also, I've realized, very beautiful) woman who's told everyone by now that her name is Magdalena, and she's originally from Sweetwater, and she started driving Greyhounds to see the world . . . well, she steps up onto the edge of the asphalt now, so she looks a little taller and in charge, and she claps to get our attention.

"Friends," she says, "great news! A new bus is here, and we're gonna get back on the road just as soon as we all load up and Mr. Dalnaut here helps transfer over all of y'all's luggage."

"All right," says Paul, next to me and sounding less serious now. "That's what I'm talking about. On the road again."

"Someone's looking after us," I answer. And then I

look at Paul and smile because we're starting over, God on our side.

He rolls his eyes at me. So. That didn't last long. I feel silly one more time.

Here's how Paul Dobbs and I left things in Loomer, Texas, so that nobody will know we're missing till we're really good and gone:

> • I left Daddy a note saying that I was going
> to the Murrays early and that I was spend-
> ing the night at Abby's afterward, so I'd see
> him tomorrow night, and I love him and he
> should have something besides a burger for
> breakfast, lunch, and dinner.

> • I sent an email to Mrs. Murray to say that I
> couldn't babysit today or tomorrow because
> I've got this overnight with Abby and then
> we're going to the water park, and I hoped
> she'd understand and could she kiss Lucy
> and Devon on the tops of their little heads
> for me? I didn't leave a voice mail for her,
> because what if she answered?

• I left nothing, no note and no email and no voice mail, for Abby. I'm just praying that nobody sees her or calls her and asks where I am, even though I'm pretty sure it's sacrilegious to pray that you don't get caught when you've done something wrong.

• Paul left a note for his parents saying that he and Dash were taking a field trip out to the flying field at the Woodlands, since the one at East Loomer Park had shut down, and they were gonna get back late and he thought he'd spend the night at Dash's afterward. So, yeah, he'd see them tomorrow.

That was my idea, the story about going off to fly planes with Dash. I thought it was a good one. Until Paul turns to me from his nice comfy blue seat on our new bus and says, "So, hey. There's really a flying field out at the Woodlands, right?"

"Oh," I answer. "Oh, mercy. I honestly don't know."

As our bus finally pulls back onto the highway and rolls farther and farther away from Loomer, I hear Mama's voice humming along underneath the rhythm of the wheels: "Not every idea is a good idea, baby. Not every idea is a good idea."

I look at Paul, who's closed his eyes, and at our backpacks shoved down by our feet, and at the broad blue sky outside. It all looks plenty promising, if you ask me.

"Hush up, Mama," I whisper. "I don't see you coming up with anything better. And also? You should talk!"

Chapter Eleven

As we step off the bus, the line that we're in sort of clumps up and slows down with everybody waiting for luggage. Paul and I didn't bring anything except for our backpacks, so we don't really have to stop, and it's a good thing too. If the Greyhound station in Loomer made me jittery and sad, the one in Houston may just knock me all the way out. It's really hot, even though we're under a great big concrete shade awning, and the buses are lined up, tight and close. Plus, there's a thick, sick smell in the air that's a mixture of oil on the pavement and bus exhaust and half-smoked cigarettes and dirt.

"Let's just keep on moving," says Paul to my back, and I try to, but people are pushing out of, like, three buses at once, and it's crowded.

I look back over my shoulder so I can actually see Paul. I want to look him in the eye to make sure he's with me. But instead what I see is a fence, a high metal fence, stretched all around us like we're in jail or something. And suddenly I feel very, very bad. Weak. Kind of hungry but kind of nauseous at the same time, with a tight sourness up near my throat.

"Our Father," I whisper automatically, like Mama might if she were here, "who art in heaven—" And just then someone presses up against me, and it's not Paul. It's a guy, and there's another guy on my left side too, and they walk with me as I walk. It's like they were waiting for my bus to arrive and they've come to pick me up.

"Got a cigarette, pretty lady?" asks the first guy, which is kind of strange, since he's holding a cigarette, or part of a cigarette, up near his mouth already.

"I'm sorry. I don't smoke," I say, and he laughs, as if that's funny. Also, he's standing really too close to me. I want to scootch away, but then I'd bump into the guy on my other side, who's shuffling along and not saying anything. He's just staring at me, which is almost worse.

I look back toward Paul again, and there are a couple of people between us now, and it's hot, and there's Cigarette Man in my face again. My heart starts to bubble like water on the stove.

"Whatcha afraid of, huh? You're a nervous little cat, aren't you?" he says, and he's right, I'm scared. I'm scared of him and his heavy plaid shirt in summer and his yellow teeth. I'm scared of being stared at and I'm scared of getting caught and I'm scared of not finding Mama. Or of finding her and she doesn't want to be found. Honestly, that would be the worst of all, wouldn't it?

I look up at Cigarette Man, actually into his eyes. I want to say, "Yes, I'm a nervous little cat and I want to get out of this line and out of this bus station and away from you. I don't know what in heaven's name I was thinking, leaving Loomer. I don't like Houston, I've never been to Florida, and I don't even know exactly where I'm going!"

But instead I say, "Excuse me." And y'know what? He steps aside. He steps aside, and I push and rush ahead, past some other folks in line and through the door into the station, where it may be cool and clean but there's the same oily smell and my heart's still flying.

"Paul," I whisper, because I've given up on getting much attention from God right now. "Paul?" And I finally find him, on his way inside, with a terrible look on his face, and I know why. Because right in front of him, there in the doorway next to Staring Guy, is a police officer.

The next thing you know, I am looking up. Up at Paul and up at clumps of people and plastic chairs and bright lights. Up from the hard, cold floor and out the windows at the awning and the buses and the high metal fence.

"What . . ." I pull myself up to sitting, but then I promptly lurch to one side and throw up. Right there on the floor of the Houston Greyhound station.

Paul squats down and hands me a red bandana that he's dipped in a water bottle. "Dang, Ivy," he says. "Are you okay? I mean, duh, no, you're not okay. Here, use this. Are you thirsty? Are you, um . . . I don't know quite what to do here."

"Oh . . . Oh, mercy . . ." I take the bandana and wipe my lips as my eyes dart around, looking for trouble. "What happened to the police officer?" I ask, because all I can think—never mind the hard, cold floor and the fainting and the throw-up and everything—is that we could be in some serious trouble here.

Paul doesn't answer. He just hands me his water and then takes his own turn looking around.

I take tiny sips like I would if I were home sick, tucked into bed with my mama tending to me. Paul uses the bandana to wipe up most of the throw-up and tosses the whole thing in the big trash bin right behind him before helping me slowly, carefully stand up.

A few folks stare at us, and one woman in a blue dress and high heels even shakes her head, like I've done something I should be ashamed of, which I guess maybe I have.

"The police officer?" I ask again, once I'm solid on my feet.

"He was just a security guard," says Paul. "He hustled those creepy guys along and he went with them. And then you fainted," he says.

"I did. I really did faint clean away," I say.

"Yeah. Wow," says Paul, and we stop talking and look straight into each other's eyes. I don't know for certain what mine look like, but Paul's look scared for the first time since we left Loomer this morning.

The plan is to do the same thing at the Houston ticket counter that we did in Loomer—buy our tickets separately, one-way, without a fuss. This time I'm going first. That's the plan. So after I catch my breath, I walk through the waiting room and out to the main lobby, where they sell tickets. I have to pass another security guard to get there, but she doesn't even look my way, and it feels pretty good being ignored. Everything would all be well and good, except that when I go for the front pocket on my pack, it's already unzipped and my money's gone. It was in there, in a little plastic pouch with a rainbow on it—a birthday gift from Kimmy. It was right there, but now it's gone!

"Hang on a sec," I say to the woman at the ticket counter. I turn around. Where is Paul? My thoughts speed up again and my hands shake. Where *is* Paul? Is he still back in the waiting room? How could my money be gone? Did it fall out when I fainted? Did I leave it on the bus? Did somebody take it? It's a lot of money—more than two hundred dollars—and I need it—*we* need it, to get out of here!

I need to go back out to where we got off the bus but there's a long line of people in the way now, waiting to go through security themselves.

"Excuse me, excuse me," I say, running past them.

I hear someone mutter, "There's a line, girl." And then the security guard says, "You're in a hurry. Ticket?" But I don't have a ticket, obviously, because I don't have any money! And she's big and stern-looking and she wears a gun.

"I lost my money," I say. "I need to get back through here and find my pouch. I . . . I . . . ."

"How about your last ticket?" she asks.

"My last ticket?"

"Yeah. Your ticket. Your receipt. If you just got off a

bus, you must have one. Otherwise, step aside." For a second I think that maybe I could run past her, but there's the big sternness and the gun, and everything in my body instantly stops and sticks, my insides and out- sides, everything as heavy as rocks. My feet push off the floor in slow motion, and I step aside. The guard turns to the next person in line, a guy who's shaking his head but not looking at me. Nobody's looking.

"The Lord is my light and my salvation," I whisper, and I swing my backpack around—my heavy-as-rocks backpack—and reach into the front pocket again—the one where my pouch is supposed to be—and there's the crumpled receipt for the ticket from Loomer to Houston, thank you God and all the angels.

"Here!" I say, a little too loudly. "Hey! Here—I found it!"

The guard nods and says, "Go on, then," and I do. I rush past the guard and through the waiting room, look- ing for a flash of familiar color on the ground—my money, the rainbow pouch—but all I see are feet and bags and empty soda bottles. The door to the outside where the buses wait is open. People are coming both in and out, and I bump up against them till I make it through. But there is just a row of identical Greyhounds out here, and I can't tell which one was ours. Maybe ours is gone.

Maybe our driver, Magdalena, is gone. I look down. I look back and around and down again.

I back up into the wall of the building and slide down, hard, until I'm sitting on the dirt-black ground. I'm back to being heavy as rocks. And from this angle it's easy to see my pouch, nearly pushed off the concrete platform. Right there, the shiny rainbow! I push up, first to my hands and knees and then to just barely standing, and I rush to the pouch, my pouch, from Kimmy. And it's empty. The zipper is wide open and the pouch is completely 100 percent empty. The money—all the money—is really and truly gone.

My eyes sting and blur, but even still, when I look around, out past the buses and through the high metal fence, I see a street sign that reads MAIN STREET. I'm not even kidding. Main Street. Main Street is supposed to be quaint. And safe. And quiet. Main Street is in Loomer, Texas, which, let's face it, is where I should be right now.

I sink back down right then and there in the middle of the pavement and drop my head into my hands. Was it those two creepy guys who took the money? The smell of buses seeps through my fingers no matter how deeply I press my face into my palms. It really doesn't matter who took it. There is nothing, not a thing in the world, I can

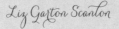

do about the smell or the heat or the money or my mama.

Pastor Lou's voice booms through my head. "I will never leave or forsake you." Ruth learned that from God, and Mama was supposed to learn it from Ruth. But she didn't. She left, and I am forsaken. I am forsaken and scared and dirty and dead broke.

"Ivy?" Paul's voice is a little too loud. It surprises me. "God, Ivy. I couldn't find you. Anywhere. You kind of freaked me out. What are you doing out here?" Paul stands in front of me holding two sodas. "You want a root beer?" he asks when I don't answer. "I was thinking it might make you feel a little better." He holds one out to me.

"It's so much worse than you know," I say. "I didn't just faint and throw up. My money's gone, Paul. Somebody took it. All of it. I don't have a dime, and we're stuck in Houston, of all places, and I don't know what on God's green earth we're gonna do."

"Oh no. Oh, God. You're kidding," says Paul. "I mean, you're not kidding, obviously. Oh, man, this sucks. What happened?" He's standing above me still, but his shoulders slouch and his head hangs.

"I don't know, really. I went to buy my ticket, but my money pouch was just plain gone. And here it is, cleaned all the way out." I hold it up as proof. "I am so, so sorry, Paul."

"Oh, God. *You're* sorry? *I'm* sorry. This whole crackpot scheme has gotten kind of out of hand. I mean, I thought it would be fun—saving your mom, seeing the space shuttle, the whole deal. I don't think I took it seriously enough." Paul drops his backpack on the concrete by my feet, cracks open his root beer, and slides down next to me.

"You thought it would be fun? You have a weird sense of adventure. Fun is hanging out at the city pool and not having homework. This wasn't supposed to be fun! This 'crackpot scheme,' as you call it, happened because we were desperate, remember? Me worrying about my mama, who's gone off missing? And you, too! You were desperate because all your dreams were being laid up in a museum. Or at least that's what you acted like, all lost and heartbroken. But it turns out you were just looking for some fun? Lordamercy, Paul Dobbs."

I gulp down my soda, icy cold and thick-sweet, not caring anymore if it hits my tummy like a brick. I deserve whatever happens from here on out. What a mighty mess.

"I will punish you according to the fruit of your doings," says the voice in my head, and I don't rightly know if it's coming from Pastor Lou, or Mama, or God himself. And it doesn't really matter, because they'd probably all be saying the same thing right about now.

Paul has enough money for two tickets. But not a whole lot more on top of that. Once we get to Florida—if we get to Florida—we won't make it long without some help from somebody, or a job at a burger joint.

"Should I just buy tickets back to Loomer and call it an aborted launch?" asks Paul. I guess he thinks he's being kind of funny with the space reference and all. We're back in the main lobby, looking over the schedule and trying to decide what to do—go ahead with our plans or turn right around and head back home.

"No," I say. "No. If we go home now, the whole thing was a bust. You sold your planes, we lied to our parents, all my babysitting money is gone—and your money's about to be gone too, once you spend it on me. And meanwhile we've got no mama, no space shuttle, no nothing to show for it all. We can't just up and go home now, can we?"

Paul doesn't answer, but by the time I look up from the schedule, he's halfway to the ticket counter. The bus to Tallahassee leaves at one thirty, and the way things are going in Houston, that's not nearly soon enough.

"Let's start thinking about how to find The Great Good Bible Church," I say to Paul. We're sitting in the front row of waiting room seats, looking out at the buses as they arrive and leave. I've got my ticket, tight in my hand. I'm done with losing things, and I'm done fighting with Paul about whether this is fun or not. I just am.

"Okay. So since we're gonna keep on going," says Paul, "here's what I think we need. A hypothesis. If your mom is really at a church in the Florida panhandle, then . . ." Paul lets his voice drag off.

"Yeah? Then, what?" I ask. But Paul doesn't answer. "Then, what? You're the scientist, Paul. You're in the business of hypotheses. You tell me!" I was hopeful for a second that he actually *had* a hypothesis, but I guess he was just prompting *me* to come up with one.

I take a big bite of one of the granola bars from my backpack, along with a last drink of root beer. I still feel wobbly after my fainting episode.

"Ivy, I know you're feeling kind of sore and mad at me," Paul says, "but I'm trying here. And d'ya have another one of those granola bars?" Which makes me feel kind of bad, because I've had my manners in hand since the first grade, and here I am drinking the root beer Paul got for me, without even thinking he might be hungry too.

"Yes. Okay. I'm sorry. Here's a bar." Paul takes it and opens it, all in one quick move. "And we're about to get back onto the bus and be squished in next to each other for about a zillion hours, right? So, truce? Truce all around?" Because now I really mean it. I'm done being mad.

"Truce," says Paul. And he holds out his hand for a fist bump. "Y'know," he says, "your Mama's missing, Ivy, but my mom and dad are pretty vacant themselves. I mean, everything's all 'Jenny, Jenny, Jenny' at my house, and I mean, I love my sister, but it sucks to be a misfit in your own family. I'm not comparing, Ivy, honest. I'm just saying. We're on the same side."

I nod and don't say a thing, because what can you say to a thing like that?

"Okay. So back to our plan," says Paul. Which is a relief. "If your mom is at a church in the Florida panhandle, then maybe one of the other churches in the Florida panhandle will have heard of it. Right? Let's start calling the ones in Tallahassee, don't you think, since that's the main city?" Paul opens a map of Florida on his lap and shows me exactly where Tallahassee is. Which makes me think he is a pretty good guy to run away with after all.

And in what seems like just minutes, a crackly voice comes over the loudspeaker announcing that our bus is boarding. The man sitting across from us crushes a cigarette with the toe of his leather boot, right there on the floor of the bus station. It wasn't lit—there are NO SMOKING signs everywhere—but he still stamps down on it like he's making sure it's good and out. And then he stands up and shakes out his skinny knees.

I wonder if he's riding with us to Florida, and also if he's overheard us, and also if he wants a granola bar. He looks like he could use one. I mean, if you look around, it seems like most folks here could use a snack. And something to drink. And a shower.

Chapter Twelve

Our new bus driver is a man with an actual uniform, and he's all kinds of proper compared to Magdalena, which makes me nervous, since we're runaways and all. He collects and punches everyone's tickets before we step up into the bus. Magdalena just had a box she held out as we passed the driver's seat. I don't think she ever even looked at the tickets. This new guy is different.

"Tallahassee?" he asks when I hand him mine. "Final destination?"

"I think so," I say, and Paul kicks at my heel a little.

"I mean, for now," I say, and Paul kicks again. I stand up taller in my shoes—I'm already tall for my age, thanks to Daddy, and I mean to look at least sixteen right this very minute.

"Yes, Tallahassee. Final destination," I say, one foot on the step of the bus.

I move ahead, and Paul gives his ticket to the driver next.

"Y'all on your own?" asks the driver to our backs, just

when I thought we were free. I stop. Paul bumps into me, and I don't feel tall. I feel tiny. Neither of us says a word for what feels like five minutes.

And then, at the same second, we both say, "Yeah."

"We're visiting our uncle," adds Paul, since I guess he figured "yeah" wasn't quite enough of an answer.

"Long ride for a couple a kids on their own," says the driver, and neither of us answers that. We move up into the bus. I'm praying we don't get asked another thing and that he just flat-out forgets we're even on the bus at all.

"Remember how we were gonna say we were visiting our grandma," I whisper to Paul once we're tucked way down in our seats, "because so many grandmas live in Florida?"

"Yep. I remember that now," says Paul. His face looks as red and hot as mine feels. We both stay low and quiet as other folks take their turns getting on the bus. Our phone calls to all the churches in Florida can wait.

It's not till the bus revs up to leave the station that I have the guts to look up and around. Sure enough, there's Skinny Man, his cigarette pack showing through his shirt pocket, brown leather boots sticking out into the aisle, kitty-corner from us. I have Mama's phone in my hand, but I'm not sure I want to make phone calls with him right there, listening.

"What if folks hear us?" I whisper to Paul, kind of nodding my head in Skinny Man's direction. Paul turns to look and busts out laughing. And then I laugh too, because in that half second since I first looked around, Skinny Man has fallen sound—and I mean sound—asleep. His mouth hangs open and his head is lopped sideways in a way that doesn't look right.

"I don't think we've got cause to worry, Ms. Green," says Paul. He's still laughing a little as he pulls a spiral notebook out of his pack and then kicks the rest of the bag underneath his seat. "Now let's get going on the research portion of our adventure."

And for a second at least, maybe even two, I think Paul is right—this *is* an adventure. And maybe there's even a tiny tidge of fun to be had. That doesn't mean we're not desperate, right? Or that we're not serious? It just means we're making the best of a bad situation.

Here's how the research portion of our adventure goes:

I open up Mama's phone.

(Yes, her phone is the kind you have to open up. The kind with actual buttons instead of a touch screen.

"Smart people shouldn't need smartphones," according to Mama.)

So I open up the phone and I dial 411, which is what smart people without smartphones do to find other people's phone numbers.

After the computer determines that I want service in English instead of Spanish, an operator answers.

"What city and state, please?"

"Tallahassee, Florida," I say.

"How can I help you?" she asks.

I pause a second and then give it a try. "Do you have the number for The Great Good Bible Church of Panhandle Florida?" I say.

"I do not," she says, which is what I expected. But I couldn't just *not ask*, could I? "Would you like another listing?" she asks, almost sounding sorry.

"Yes," I say. "Yes. I guess I'm looking for a Baptist church."

"I find a number of Baptist churches," says the operator. And then she lists them. "Bradfordville First Baptist Church. Celebration Baptist Church. First Baptist Church. Highpoint Baptist Church. Immanuel Baptist Church . . ." She goes on and on, in alphabetical order. I scrawl them down in Paul's spiral notebook as quick as I

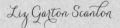

can. I mean, my handwriting's barely legible even when I'm sitting at a school desk, and this bus is no help at all.

"Would you like the number for one of the churches I've listed?" asks the operator, and I say, "Yes, I'll try First Baptist Church." I just say that 'cause it seems like "First" is a good place to start.

And then a computer connects me. My face flushes hot, and I lick my lips and the bus rolls on as I listen to the phone ring at the First Baptist Church in Tallahassee, Florida. We are heading in that direction, I think, but we don't even know if that's where we want to be.

"Greetings," says the voice on the other end of the line. "First Baptist."

"Oh, um, well, hi," I say.

Dear God, I did not expect someone to pick up the phone.

"May I help you, ma'am?" she says, which makes me less panicky because she apparently thinks I'm a grown-up!

"Yes, I hope so. We're looking for a church. The Great Good Bible Church of Panhandle Florida," I say. And the woman doesn't say anything when I pause. So to help her out, I say, "We were wondering if you know of it."

"Is it in Tallahassee?" she asks. But before she lets me answer, she says, "It can't be in Tallahassee, 'cause I would've heard of it, and I've never heard of it."

"Oh. Well. Okay, thanks."

It's discouraging, during the research portion of an adventure, to hang up without any new information at all. And, especially, to repeat this *particular* portion of the research portion again and again. I call back and ask the operator to connect me to Immanuel Baptist Church. And then Northwoods Baptist Church, which I think is kind of funny since we're in the South. And then Maranatha. And as I talk to the church secretaries, Paul crosses off the names of the churches, one by one. The secretaries all pretty much tell me the same thing: they've never heard so much as a whisper about The Great Good Bible Church. Not a whisper. One woman says, "I haven't the foggiest, young lady," which I guess means I'm not that grown-up sounding after all. "The Great Good Bible Church doesn't even sound Baptist, if you ask me," she says. And I kinda think she's got a point.

A couple of the ladies are extra nice, though. One says she's never heard of The Great Good but we are always welcome to visit *her* church—"It's where God's people gather," she says. And another invites me to be a part of their cozy flock. "Like a lamb coming in from the cold," she says. And I promise you, I'm not just gone-off crazy, her voice sounds a bit like Mama's. I've half a mind to head straight there. Like a little lamb.

Paul finally makes a couple of calls for me, because I'm about this far from giving up, but he gets the same answer. The Great Good Bible Church may as well not even exist.

My mind races straight past possibility and heads toward hopelessness. What if we go all this way and don't find Mama? What if Mama doesn't want to be found, at least by us? What if she's not just gone for the summer but gone for good?

I shake my head like a wet dog would, and I sit up straight. "I'll finish up," I say to Paul. "I'd rather have something to do." And as I reach for the phone, I look around to make sure we're still speaking in private. Skinny Man's mouth hangs open, and he hasn't budged a bit.

"Can you connect me to Highpoint Baptist Church in Tallahassee, Florida," I say to the operator, and while it rings, I whisper to Paul, "What's our next plan?"

"Pardon me?" says a man on the other end of the line.

"Oh. Oh, gosh. I'm sorry. I was talking to someone here. Listen, you don't know of a place called The Great Good Bible Church of Panhandle Florida, do you?"

"The Great Good Bible Church. I don't think so. Why?"

Why? Well, huh. Nobody's asked me that before. I swallow, and then, because he's got a nice voice—about as much like Daddy's as the little lamb woman's was like Mama's—I start talking. Like he's my own personal pastor.

"Well, sir, this is all kind of crazy," I say. "The thing is, I'm looking for The Great Good Bible Church and this Holy Roller preacher called Hallelujah Dave because I'm pretty sure—almost one hundred percent positive, actually—that that's where my mama is. She needs her medication. And I need her."

"Oh," says the Daddy-like man on the other end of Mama's cell phone.

And that's all he has time to say, because I start up again. "And I'm on my way to bring her home. But I can't very well do that if I can't find her, can I?" That's what I say into the phone, and that's when I feel Paul touch my arm with his fingertips. I turn to look at him, and he's holding one finger up to his lips, as a *shh* sign. But not in a mean way like this morning. This time it's almost gentle, really.

And then I look across at Skinny Man, and guess what? He's staring straight at me too.

117

"No, I guess you can't," says the voice I forgot was there. "That would make it pretty tough," he says. "But I have something for you, my dear. I don't know The Great Good Bible Church, but Hallelujah Dave I've heard of. Just this morning. He was in the Tallahassee paper, and I hate to tell you this, but that man's in jail. I don't know where that puts your mama, but the fellow who calls himself Hallelujah Dave is most definitely in the county jail."

Jail. Jail? My throat stops up, and I drop the phone into my lap like it's on fire. I hear a murky, spooky voice calling out, "Miss? Miss, are you okay?" But it's Paul who reaches for the phone and says "Thank you for your help" before hanging up properly. Which is only right, because the pastor from Highpoint Baptist truly *was* a help. Just not the kind of help I expected. Or wanted, really.

Chapter Thirteen

I sit, stone silent, for a while, my eyes kind of burning from looking out the window at everything flying by.

Hallelujah Dave's in jail. I cannot believe that this is what's become of my mama's life, or mine. We are good stock, or at least that's what she always says. If one of us isn't feeling right about something, like when Daddy's roofing business suffered and we had to "tighten our belts," she'd say, "Don't you worry, honey. We are good stock. This is a bump in the road, but we are good stock and we'll be fine. You can have faith in that." And we always did.

But at some point I guess Mama stopped believing it herself. It's like the cross around my neck. The shine wore right off, and suddenly Mama was hurling herself onto the floor of a strange church at a strip mall and crawling all the way to Florida with a guy who goes and gets himself thrown into jail.

I rub the cross. I like it. It's familiar. But my mama? I don't even know who my mama is anymore.

"Ivy. You're shivering," says Paul. "And you haven't said a word in miles. You're making me kind of nervous. Seriously. C'mon. What's up?"

I pull my knees up under my T-shirt and squeeze my arms around them, making myself warmer and warmer and tighter and tighter and littler and littler. I squeeze and squeeze, like I might make myself disappear. But no matter how little I get, I'm still here, and so is this truth:

"Hallelujah Dave is in jail," I say.

"Wow," says Paul. "Okay, wow. Yeah. Well, that's a heck of a clue," he says, kind of shocked. But from the looks of the little twitch in the left corner of his mouth, he still thinks this is kind of an adventure. Maybe that should make me mad, but honestly? I can't help but thank God for that little twitch.

A Greyhound bus does not, it turns out, go straight from Houston to Tallahassee. It stops bunches of times, in places that are all at least half as creepy as Houston. Sometimes you just want to get to the place you're going.

We mostly stay on the bus at the stops, though Paul gets off once because there's a food stand right outside and he is starving. I keep thinking that the less I do—the less I eat, the fewer times I weave down the bus aisle to the bathroom—the quicker we'll get to where we're going. Plus, I lost my starving-ness somewhere between home and here.

But it's then, when Paul gets off the bus to buy a po'boy sandwich in Baton Rouge, Louisiana, that Skinny Man decides to lean across the aisle and talk to me. I am telling you, if this had happened this morning, I would've screamed or fainted or, God forbid, thrown up again. But this morning was a long time ago. So I look straight at him and say, "Can I help you?"

"I doubt it," he says, "but I might be able to help you." He stops and coughs and chokes on whatever's in his lungs. He really doesn't seem like the helping sort. "I heardja talking, and it seems like someone you know is in some trouble. And I just happen to know a thing or two about jail."

Mmm-hmm. I'll bet he does. Oh, mercy me. Why am I not surprised?

"Yeah?" I say.

"You kids aren't gonna get anywhere, nosing around a cop shop," he says. "They're gonna be more interested in getting the lowdown on *you* than giving you the lowdown on the guy you're looking for. I can guaran-dang-tee you that."

It's hard to look straight into his eyes because the bus is dark and he makes me nervous, but I can feel in my bones that he's right. We are just a couple of kids with T-shirts and backpacks. Even when we're trying to be all mature, we look like we should be in school, not in jail. We just plain do, and thank goodness for that, I guess, but it's a fact that is not gonna be helpful at all in these circumstances.

So by the time Paul gets back onto the bus, I've arranged to go with Ricky, which is Skinny Man's name, to the Leon County Jail. It turns out he knows exactly where it is—again, not a big surprise—and that he's got to head to that part of town when he hits Tallahassee anyway.

"I owe a lot of folks some kindnesses," is how he put it, "but most of 'em won't have none of it, and I can't blame 'em. Giving you guys a hand, it's just something I can do."

Here's the thing. I don't want to trust him, I promise you that. A smoky, scary, skinny-looking guy who knows way too much about jail than anyone ought to? No, thank you. But honest to goodness, what choice do I have? So I arranged it. I arranged it for me, and I guess I went ahead and arranged it for Paul, too.

"He'll be like our guide or our chaperone or something," I say, and Paul looks at me like the crazy that my mama has might be catching. But he doesn't *say* anything like that. He just reaches across the aisle to shake Ricky's hand.

"Nice to meet you, man," Paul says, which proves once and for all that he might be the nicest and most flexible guy on earth.

Paul really *would've* made the perfect astronaut, what with how he adjusts to unexpected surprises.

He doesn't even jump or panic when my phone—well, Mama's phone, actually—starts to ring. It's not technically even a "ring," I guess. It's a birdsong. Mama's birdsong, the tone she chose because it made her feel like it was a new morning every time it rang. The birdsong she left at home with us when she took off on her adventure.

And I guess that's when it first occurs to me—what if Mama left because she needed an adventure? Like Paul? Or even like me?

Here's the thing I like best about cell phones: caller ID. When I pull Mama's ringing phone out of my backpack to see who's calling, the screen says *HOME*. Which means Daddy's figured out that I'm gone and that I have Mama's phone. I picture him standing in the kitchen with his work boots on, both me and Mama missing now. It's a sorry thought. But even as much as I love my daddy, I don't answer.

By eleven at night Daddy's left four voice mails, and they all kind of say the same thing. "Ivy. Baby. I love you. And I'm not mad but I am worried. I'd like to come and get you, so could you just let me know where you are?"

And then there's always a little something about Mama, something like, "I'm sorry I didn't talk to you more about your mama leaving. I was trying to stay strong, baby. I was trying to keep you safe."

Or "Your mama's a grown-up, Ivy Green, so she has to look after herself. But it's *my* job to look after you!"

Or "Gosh darn it, Ivy. I'm holding your mother responsible for this." His voice cracks during that last one, which about splits me open and makes me want to dial him back, I feel so bad. But I don't. I can't.

"We are not traveling a zillion miles in a smelly, dirty, tin can of a bus just to get hauled home by our parents before we even hit Florida," I say when Paul asks what I'm going to do about the messages.

"Hey! That's the way! Ladies and Gentlemen, I'd like to introduce Ivy Green with Spunk," says Paul, sounding like a sports announcer on TV. "Ivy Green with Spunk."

And I know it sounds silly, but I feel kind of proud when he says it. Maybe "Spunk" could be my middle name. Ha! Can you imagine what Mama'd say about that? Ivy Spunk Green. Talk about kooky!

I turn off the phone and stow it deep in my backpack, wad my sweatshirt into a sort of pillow, curl up against the window, and go to sleep for another bit. When I wake next, it's pitch dark both inside and outside, and really cold from the A/C. And, news flash, now I *am* starving.

"I figured you'd get hungry sometime." Paul pulls a foil-wrapped fried-oyster sandwich out of his sweatshirt pocket and hands it to me. It is somehow still a little warm, the bun soft, the oysters crispy and spicy. I eat the whole thing in a few bites.

"So I guess your God didn't do too good a job looking after old Hallelujah Dave, did he?" Paul says as I finish eating, just as I was starting to like him again. As a friend, I mean. But still, he has to go and ruin it.

"He's not 'my God,' Paul Dobbs. He's all of ours—even mean boys like you. So there. God works in mysterious ways. You know that as well as I do. Don't pretend you've never spent a day in church. How do you know God wasn't protecting Mama? If Hallelujah Dave is in jail, maybe he belongs there. Maybe it's safer for everyone." I pause to take a big breath and shake off my sleep a little. "Sheesh," I say. "You are what Pastor Lou would call a tribulation, you know that?"

And then I add, "But thank you for the po'boy." Because I was raised right.

"Oh, Ivy! Hang on a second. I was kidding around. Y'know, joking? It's something normal kids do when they've run away from home and are on their way to a jailhouse in Florida. It helps pass the time and clear the air and all that." Paul sighs, like *I'm* the one who's saying wrongheaded things, not him. And here's a crazy thing: for a split second Paul looks just like my daddy looks when he's disappointed in me.

I go back to staring out my window even though I can't see much, thanks to the night and the speed and the fact that my eyes are bleary and tired and sore. Even the stars in the black, black sky are a blur. Paul would probably like looking out at them, but of course he gave me the window seat, just to be sweet.

So here I am—Miss Thoughtless Runaway Girl with No Mama, No Middle Name, and No Sense of Humor, the Girl Who's Disappointed Everybody—sitting spoiled in the window seat as we cross the state line and drive smack into the great-good panhandle of Florida.

❦

"The Big Dipper," I say, sort of lurching back into myself as the familiar constellations suddenly appear right above us.

"Huh?" says Paul. His voice is croaky and tired.

"I just saw the Big Dipper. It was kind of nice to see something I recognized," I say into the quiet bubble of the bus. "I thought maybe you'd want to see it too."

I know that kind of sounds like I'm trying to make up with him, but really, it's so dark that I think I'm sort of pretending that it's not even Paul I'm talking to. Maybe it's Daddy, Abby, Mama, or God.

"Oh, yeah, Ursa Major. You know that the Big Dipper is just a little part of a bigger constellation, right? Ursa Major, the mama bear?"

Nope. It's definitely Paul after all. The expert.

"Um, okay," I say. "How do you know that?"

Paul leans into me a little so he's got a better view out the bus window.

"Well, I was really kind of into star stories for a while. Y'know, the myths?"

"Yeah," I say, "that figures."

If you stare long enough, Ursa Major and all the other stars in the sky become a fast bright blur—a fast bright quiet lonely blur.

127

After a minute or two I say, "I guess you know star stories better than you know Bible stories, probably."

"They're not all that different, really," Paul answers. "I mean, Ursa Major and Ursa Minor are a mother and a child. They've been through all sorts of terrible stuff, including getting turned into bears, but they end up right next to each other forever in the sky. Doesn't that sound like the sort of ending you'd get in the Bible?"

I don't know for sure if Paul's being sweet with me or snarky. And I'm not sure it matters, 'cause as all the stars in the universe fly by, all I can think is, *Even that little baby star bear has his mother.*

ail isn't what you'd expect it to be. I mean, it should be super-scary, right? Loud and dark and super-scary. But walking into the Leon County Jail isn't that much different from walking into the lobby of a school or a doctor's office, and it's a whole heap better than certain bus stations I know.

The place is actually clean and bright, and the soda machine spits out cold bottles of soda, which we all need. We traveled straight through the night, folded up with crinks in our necks and tingles in our feet, and then barely took time to splash our faces in the restroom at the Tallahassee Greyhound station before getting on a city bus that brought the three of us here, right here, to the Leon County Jail. Where it feels good just to stand still for a second, on this solid, polished floor, instead of flying sixty miles an hour through the dark.

Besides jail, here's another thing that's different than you'd expect—Ricky. It turns out Ricky had a clean collared shirt in his pack, and a comb, and a breath mint or something. It's like he's a new man. Literally, I guess, since now he's pretending to be the faithful stepbrother of Davey Floyd Roman. (Davey Floyd Roman being Hallelujah Dave to you and me. We found out his real name in yesterday's paper that we scrounged up at the bus station this morning.)

I'm darn near believing in Ricky-the-stepbrother myself, that's how good and true he looks and seems. Now we just need to convince the police.

"Oh dear, dear God," I whisper as Ricky walks up to the front desk, "I am so sorry about all these lies and the running away from home and everything. I hope you can forgive me since it really and truly is all in the name of doing the right thing."

I feel Paul Dobbs's shoulders rise up and sink back down with a slow deep breath, right next to me as I pray. We haven't said much to each other since late last night, but there hasn't been much to say since Ricky kind of stepped in as our grown-up.

"And please forgive Paul, too," I whisper. "Not one bit of this is his fault. He's just trying to help." That last part I whispered a tidge louder, on purpose, thinking maybe Paul would hear it and accept it as my apology for being all itchy with him—last night and all the way along, really. Plus, I figure he isn't talking to God himself, so he could use the support.

The policeman on duty is actually a really pretty police*woman* with long pink nails that click on her keyboard when she types. Ricky smiles at her as he says hello.

"We're here to see Davey Floyd Roman," he says, plain as day, as if we have all the right in the world to be marching into jail and asking to meet with a prisoner today.

"Did you come to pick him up?" asks the policewoman. *Click, click, click.*

"Pick him up? Uh, no. That wasn't exactly the plan. Why?"

"Oh, I thought you might be with the ministry sent to get him. He's been bailed out, and I'm just completing the paperwork now." She looks up at Ricky, her pink-tipped fingers still in place in front of her, her badge big and shiny over her heart.

I watch as Ricky shifts his weight from one skinny leg to the other and takes a second before saying whatever he's gonna say next. This wasn't what we'd counted on, Davey Floyd checking out of jail before we even got in to see him. If he leaves now, we'll have to start from scratch in finding Mama. He's our best and only hope, this crazy-crooked preacher in prison. If that's not the most ridiculous fix to be in. I take a gulp of soda to calm my nerves.

"Well, hey, that's great," says Ricky, calm as calm can be. "I'm his stepbrother, just here to check on him. I know he needs all the help he can get from the Lord God Almighty, so really, it's great about the ministry. Can we just get one quick word with him before he leaves?"

Oh, yes, please and thank you, I think. *Yes, please and thank you, Skinny Ricky.*

"It's quiet in here this morning," says the policewoman, looking at Ricky, and then at us, and then around the otherwise empty room. "If y'all will just slide down to the end of this counter, I'll bring him out and you can talk while I finish things up and get him ready to roll."

Ricky turns around with a great big grin for me and Paul, and my heart starts to settle. See what I mean about Ricky being different than you'd expect? He may be a tired, skinny, yellow-toothed guy, but it turns out he sure is someone you can count on in the Leon County Jail.

But now, staring straight across the wide white countertop at Davey Floyd Roman, I change my mind about the scariness. Jail *is* scary after all, just like you'd think. It's cold, and way too bright, and the prisoners wear prisoner clothes. But here we are anyway, with nowhere else to be or go, and if this man in orange is the way to my mama, then here is where we simply have to be.

"Stepbrother, huh?" Davey Floyd says through his teeth, without even opening his mouth, like he's a creepy ventriloquist or something. He's talking to Ricky, I guess, about faking that they're relatives, but he's looking right at me, maybe 'cause I'm smack in the middle of his little group of visitors, or maybe because I'm the only girl or something, but yeah, it's kind of scary. And his eyes? They are fake blue, like they're glass stones instead of eyes, and his hair is long and blond and tied back in a sort of bun.

A preacher with a big blond bun, I kid you not.

Honestly, Mama, for all the good on this green earth, what were you thinking?

"I didn't have the heart to tell 'em I don't *have* a step-brother," Davey Floyd says, sarcastic, but still low and teethy, probably so as not to get the officer's attention, "because I just hate to ruin someone's fun. And plus, I was curious 'bout who'd be visiting a fallen son of God in the county clink. So. Here I am. You got me, probably right where you want me. Everybody's got me, from the sounds of things. The snake-mad folks from Florida and

133

Alabama and Texas and Tennessee. As if it's all my fault that the dumb and devout are nearly desperate to give away their money. Like I can help it if I was in the right place at the right time, if you know what I mean. Used to be it was a person's own responsibility to look after their money . . ."

It is as if he's never gonna stop talking, in his quiet, sarcastic, angry preacher voice. I think this must be what sucked Mama in, this voice rolling on and on like a train, till a person has no choice but to up and follow it to Florida.

"I mean, far be it from me to not help people out," Davey Floyd goes on. "As we all know, the word of God is the word of God is the word of our Almighty high heavenly host in the sky, no matter who's speaking it. You can't fault me for that, for passing on the good news and the warnings, now can you? A man's got to do his called-for work. The Lord asks that of us all. So then, that said, Hallelujah Dave at your service. How can I help you?"

And finally he comes to a full stop, like a car at a school zone crosswalk. But we just stand there, the three of us, staring back at him with our mouths open. Open like nets for catchin' bugs, Mama would say, not sure if he's finished, for one thing, and not sure what to say in response, for another. So the pause is a long one.

But then I start talking back at him, not even really meaning to. I mean, I may be scared of the Leon County Jail and also scared of this glassy-eyed, bun-haired preacher man, but I guess I'm more scared of never finding my mama ever again.

"Mr. Roman, um, sir," I say, "I don't rightly know what's going on here, and I guess that's between you and God and the sheriff anyhow. And I don't know a thing about all those angry church folks you're talking about . . ." I stop to take in a breath of air-conditioned air and to catch a sideways look at the police lady on the other side of the room. She is still busy with her computer and tapping fingernails, and now she's on the telephone, too. I twist the little cross at my neck with a whisper of thanks for her distraction, and right then Hallelujah Dave opens his mouth like he's about to start talking again. But I don't let him. I just keep on going, 'cause I can be a train too, Mr. Hallelujah. You just watch.

"But I'm pretty sure you know Diana Green? From Loomer, Texas? She followed you to The Great Good Bible Church of Panhandle Florida, and I'm not sure why, because she already *had* a church, and a home, and a husband, and a daughter. And that's who I happen to be, Mr. Roman. Diana Green's daughter. She's my mama.

Did you know that? Did you know any of that when you got her to go with you to Florida?" I stop to take another breath, but my voice isn't shaking anymore, and now I feel a lot more mad than scared.

But y'know who *does* look scared? Mr. Hallelujah Davey Floyd Roman with the glassy eyes. He looks shocked, and scared, and now *his* mouth hangs open like a net for catchin' bugs. And it seems like he might be done train-talking for a while, because he doesn't say a single thing.

I look a little to my left at Ricky, standing back with his arms crossed, and a little to my right at Paul, who's leaning forward into the countertop. They both look like they're waiting for something to happen next. But nothing happens. Not a thing. And the four of us just stand still together in this too-cold room, like we're lights hanging from the ceiling. That's what it feels like, like we are all hanging lights with those tiny chain pull cords, and we are waiting, waiting, still and dark.

And then, right at the very second when I think I might die of quiet, Paul stands up straight and says, "I believe Ivy was talking to you, Mr. Roman. We'd like some answers about her mama, if you please. Like, where is she?"

And I know this is inappropriate seven ways from Sunday, but I could kiss Paul Dobbs, right here and now, for this tiny gift of grace.

"Right. Yep. Diana Green," answers Hallelujah Dave. His voice is different. Normal. Less low and preachery. Not like a train. Not through his teeth. And I'm pretty sure his Southern accent is gone.

He laughs sort of a sad, head-shakey, chuckley laugh. "Yeah, I know her," he says straight to me. "She's one of the folks who's maddest at me, I guess." He blinks his eyes about three times fast—looking either startled or nervous or both—and I wait for him to say something more.

But before he can, the pretty jailer walks over with her heels *click, click, click*ing on the hard floor, just the same way her fingernails clicked the keyboard. "Okay, folks. So that'll do it," she says, like everything's fine and normal over here. "Let's wrap it up. I'm ready to take you back, get you your things, and get you out of here, Mr. Roman. The legal rep from, um . . ."—she looks down at her clipboard—"from the Ministry of Heavenly Love," she says, "is gonna be here to get you in just a sec." She motions to Davey Floyd to follow her, and he kind of coughs to clear his throat, and then turns, like he's gonna do what she says, like he's all finished with business here,

"Wait! Wait just one second! Where is my mama, mister? Don't you take one more step till you tell me where she is!" The words come out shaky, but loud and clear, because I did not run away to Florida and lie my way into a county jail just to hang out with a creepy preacher for a few minutes and leave with no information at all.

Davey turns back toward us and leans toward me. It is dead quiet except for the hum from the soda machine, and we hold our breaths. Even the policewoman seems to want to hear his answer, but we very nearly miss it, all of us, because Davey Floyd Roman's voice is suddenly nearly a whisper.

"She's in the hospital," he says, and that's when I swing my hand out across the counter, to grab him or scratch him or maybe hit him. But I'm not tall enough and the counter's too wide, and Hallelujah Dave just turns and walks away.

Our policewoman, you can tell, doesn't have the faintest idea what to do next, seeing as how things have gotten a little bit out of hand. And I suddenly see how she's almost a teenager herself, all long hair and fingernails and just the big badge to indicate she's supposed to be in charge around here.

"Wait here," she says to Paul and Ricky and me, kind of desperately, and she rushes Hallelujah Dave from the room.

"*Don't* wait. Scoot!" whispers Ricky, and we do. We slide across the slick floor, dragging our backpacks and our soda bottles with us. Then we push through the heavy glass door, and we go. In no more than about five seconds, the three of us are two blocks down and around the corner. Safe. I am panting and tripping a little and dropping my pack. And, to top off everything, I have the weirdest and most desperate urge to laugh.

"You, little lady, were cut out for this," says Ricky. Which does make me laugh, for real, and then Paul and Ricky join me. We are laughing, doubled-over fools on the corner of Appleyard Drive and Municipal Way in Tallahassee, Florida, and it feels just fine.

There is more than one hospital in Tallahassee, so it takes a few calls, but we do it. We find my mama. She is a confirmed and official patient at Tallahassee Memorial Hospital. In this, at least, Hallelujah Dave didn't lie.

"Okay," I say. "It's really okay. We found her. She may be in the hospital, but we found her and it's gonna be okay." I'm kinda crouching down on the gray curb, but there's a shade tree over us, which is why we stopped here to make the calls. I lean back and close my eyes for a second. I can't believe we did it.

"Well, I'm guessin' my work here is done," says Ricky, and as I open my eyes again, I see him reach out to shake Paul's hand, and then mine.

"Peace be with you," I sort of accidentally say as we clasp. I can't help it—it's an automatic thing, from church.

"And also with you," says Ricky, like it's automatic for him, too, if you can believe that. Skinny Ricky—a church-goer, of all things. Which makes me think, no wonder he helped us, never mind his shady past. I have half a mind to say, right then and there, "See, Paul Dobbs? God *was* watching out. For all of us." But I don't, because I, Ivy Blank Green, am turning over a new leaf where Paul Dobbs is concerned. A leaf of kindness. So instead of say-ing a single thing, I just reach up to Ricky and follow our handshake with a hug. And he hugs me back with a sort of pat, pat, pat on my back like Daddy might do.

It's after he turns to go and I plop back down with Paul that I have a good look at the phone in my hands. The voice mail light is blinking green again.

vy, it's Daddy. Listen, honey. We know you're in Florida, thanks to the cell phone company. And we know that Paul Dobbs is with you, or at least we're pretty sure about that, since he's not where he said he'd be or with who he said he'd be with, and you guys have struck up a friendship, I guess. So anyway, here's what I want you to do, baby. I want you to stay put. I'm coming. I'm coming to get you. And everything's gonna be fine. But in the meantime, Ives, if you wanted to give me a ring?" His voice trails off then, so I just barely hear how he says "I love you, honey" at the end.

"Oh, God. Oh no!" I say, with the phone still pressed up to my ear. "That was my daddy again. He knows where I am, and he knows you're here too, and he's on his way. Here—to Florida! I'm serious. We are good and caught, and probably in a massive heap of trouble, too."

I shut up to listen as the second message plays. It's Abby this time. "I know you told your daddy you were at my house," she says, "even though you weren't, and I'm not mad, not a bit, Ivy, but I am kind of scared. Where are you? Could you send me a sign—a text or something? I promise I won't give you away to anyone. I just really, really want to know if you're okay." She actually sounds like she's crying a little bit, and Abby hardly ever cries. I swallow hard, and the phone beeps again.

"Ivy. It's Mrs. Murray. Your daddy gave me this number. We hope you're getting these messages, sweetheart. What matters is that you know we love you. Life is a funny, changing thing, Ivy. You just got caught up in the river of life this summer, that's all. But underneath that rushing water is all of us, loving you, so let the currents pull you back home, Ivy. We are missing you here."

"Oh, Paul. What have we done?" I bring the phone down into my lap and fold my hands around it. But Paul doesn't answer. He's not looking at me. He's leaning back and looking up at a sky that's crisscrossed with two long white jet contrails, one going one way, one going the other. I look with him and start to breathe again.

"Ivy," Paul finally says, when a good minute's gone by, "we've got a good reason for being here, right? And your daddy, he seems like the kind of guy who understands a good reason. Right?" Paul looks calm, like his answer solves everything.

But the thing is, even if he's right as rain, it doesn't fix the fact that Daddy's on his way to Florida, we don't have Mama yet, and this whole crazy scheme might be as good as over right now.

"What about your parents?" I ask. "What are they gonna say about all this?"

Paul shrugs. "They're sort of reasonable to the power of ten. Like, so reasonable, they're almost dead half the time. I don't worry too much about them." Which should be a relief—one thing we don't need to worry about—but Paul's voice sounds kind of sad. Almost like he wished he *did* have to worry, at least a little.

With my thumb I press and hold the button to power down the phone. I'm still not ready to call anybody back. I don't know what I'm ready for, and I guess neither does Paul, 'cause we just sit, still and quiet. Even in the shade it's hot, and my legs stick to the earth and the concrete, and my ankles look puffy and dirty, and my stomach is starting to growl. A girl can get to feeling kind of hopeless in the middle of summer in the panhandle of Florida when she's spent the morning in jail, discovered that her mama's in the hospital, and freaked out pretty near everyone who loves her.

"Okay, Ivy," says Paul, who is just plain good at

knowing when to break a silence. "We can't just sit here till your dad arrives. I'm thinking it won't be that bad in the end. Any of it. I mean, he's gonna be glad we're okay, right?" he says. "And plus, we've found your mom. Mission accomplished!"

"No, I don't think it really is gonna be okay," I say, right along with the creaky rumble of my stomach. "We may have technically found Mama, but she's in the hospital, of all places—and we don't even know why. My daddy's headed this way, chasing us down like a bounty hunter. And, to top it all off, we're not even close to making it to Cape Canaveral to see the space shuttle. Which, by the way, was supposed to be the fun part of the trip—*your* part of the trip. Turns out you didn't need to come at all, since I've just been wasting your time, tracking Hallelujah Dave and ditching the police and whatever other crazy and possibly illegal stuff I've gotten us into. I mean, honestly. This whole thing is turning out to be kind of a raw deal," I say.

"Awright, well, here's the thing. It's only a raw deal if we give up now. I mean, that would be a total bummer. 'Cause then we ran away and ticked off our parents for nothing. Wasn't it you who had the motto about every day being full of ideas or something? Y'know, for Mrs. Murray? So let's come up with an idea. Come on!"

I turn my hot, filthy self to face Paul. "You remember my motto?"

"Well, um, sort of. I mean, I think so. I remember it was a good one. We all thought so." Paul swallows a big noticeable lump in his throat. "Remind me what it was, exactly?"

"Every good day starts with an idea," I say.

And right as I say that, I have one.

We figure out that you can pretty much go straight across the city of Tallahassee on the Azalea Route, which for some reason makes me feel better, since it sounds so sweet and mild. And you can do the whole thing for $1.25, which Paul calls a worthy investment for "a couple of fugitives about to attempt a break-in at the local hospital."

He's trying to make me a little less nervous by making me laugh. What we're *actually* gonna attempt, though, is a break*out* not a break-in. We're gonna go get my mama before my daddy gets us. At least that's the idea.

So we're standing here at the bus stop, sort of half-laughing about our plan, when this dog comes running toward us, barking up a storm, like it's his job to guard the place. But he's big and goofy and floppy, sort of reddish with white paint splotches—a big goofy floppy dog, just like the kind I want—and he's wearing a sweater! Which would be kind of funny anyway, but especially in Florida in the middle of summer, of all things.

He's barking and barking, and Paul yells, "Hey!" I guess to scare the dog away, but Paul is clearly the one who's scared. He backs up and presses himself into the corner of the little bus shelter and says "Hey" again, but quieter this time.

"Come 'ere, pup," I say. "Come 'ere." And then I do that clicking thing with my tongue that dogs love, and sure enough, he stops barking and turns away from Paul and toward me.

"Ivy, watch out," says backed-into-the-corner Paul, even though the dog is now rubbing his head into my hands and practically purring.

"Paul, he's wearing a *sweater*," I say, and now I'm really actually laughing at the idea of a big goofy floppy dog in a sweater being dangerous.

And then I hear some guy yell, "Sammy! Sammy, come!" And Sammy turns on a dime and heads toward home. I give Paul a full-on grin as he steps out of the corner of the shelter, and when the bus rolls up, I hop up the steps feeling better than I've felt in a couple of days, 'cause there is just nothing like a dog. I look back at Paul, and he's looking back himself, probably making sure that Sammy really did go home.

Tallahassee Memorial sits like a huge, white cube at the corner of Miccosukee and Centerville Roads. It is nothing like the pretty little hospital in Loomer, with a lawn that's lined with flowerbeds and statues of children. This hospital does not seem like a nice place to get well, is what I mean, which makes me even readier than I was before to go on up there and get my mama out.

There's a couple of big, heavy glass doors to get into the lobby. I lead the way, and Paul follows. The big clock on the wall reads ten forty-five. No wonder I'm starving, since all I've had today is a soda, and not much last night either. And, also, looking at the clock makes me wonder how soon Daddy'll be here. Is he driving or flying? Or is he taking the bus, like we did? What I wish is that he'd decided to walk his way to Florida so we could have a teeny bit more time to work this whole thing out.

A woman sits at an information desk in the lobby, and I head straight for her. Paul splits off and walks into the gift shop that's lined with balloons and stiff stuffed animals. Stiff stuffed animals are more for display than something a person would really want to cuddle. When I was seven, I won one—a stiff bunny—in a ball toss at the Loomer County Fair. According to the way Mama and Daddy tell it, I was so disappointed that I gave the bunny back to the man at the booth and said, "Shame on you." I still get teased about it, but honestly, nobody on God's green earth deserves a stiff stuffed animal, least of all the sick folks in a hospital.

"How may I help you today?" asks the woman at the desk. She wears green scrubs, and her badge says, *My name is Constance*. She looks like she's Mama's age. She actually looks kind of like Mama, with her long, pretty neck and soft cheeks and glossy hair pulled back like that. Only this lady's life is probably normal as nails. She's here volunteering while her daughter goes to summer camp or something, and probably their dinner's already in the slow cooker at home.

"Can I have the room number for Mrs. Diana Green, please?" My heart flutters as Constance taps away at the computer. I half-expect her to tell me that Mama's gone, but she doesn't.

She just says, "Head on up to three north, doll. That's for cardiac care. Room 312. The nurses up there will show you the way."

"Third floor it is." Paul's voice startles me. I didn't realize he'd stepped back beside me. He slips a banana and a bag of pretzels into my hand as we head for the elevator. "C'mon, Ivy Blank Green. Let's go get your mama," he says. And I have to admit, I don't mind my lonely little nickname so much when Paul says it.

On the third floor when we ask for directions, a nurse called Nan says, "Oh, I can take you to Mrs. Green." And the next thing you know, here we are, standing in front of room 312. I can see, through the open door, a pair of feet on the bed, in fuzzy socks. Mama's feet, I can tell already.

Chapter Sixteen

"Knock, knock, Mrs. Green," says Nan. "I've got visitors for you!" She moves through the doorway toward the fuzzy feet, and I follow, my own breath noisy in my ears. Paul is right behind me—I can hear his breath too, slower and softer than my own. And then there she is, my mama, lying stock-still upon the bed, with her eyes closed. She's dressed in a lavender jogging suit and the fuzzy socks, and there's a thin blanket partway covering her belly and chest. She looks smaller than usual, and pale, and I can't help myself, not for one second longer. I push past Nan and rush up against the side of the bed.

"Mama!" I say. "Mama, it's me," and before the words are even fully out of my mouth, Mama opens her eyes and turns her head toward me.

"Oh, Ivy," she says, in her same old Mama voice that I know and love. "Oh, baby doll."

She looks me straight in the eye, and it's almost too much for me to bear. I sort of sit-fall into the chair by the head of the bed, and Mama reaches out for me, just as Paul pats one hand very softly on my shoulder from behind. My head falls forward, and I hear Nan scootch herself out of the room, which is best, because if I completely lose it, it won't be in public (though having Paul here is bad enough).

But it turns out I don't cry. I just sit there with my head down, and I breathe and shake. I don't know if I'm upset or relieved or tired or scared. I don't know what I am besides all wrung out, and maybe it doesn't even matter. It's just been weeks and weeks since I've seen my mama, is all.

So I breathe and shake, and Mama holds on to me and whispers, "Ivy, Ivy," over and over again.

"Mama," I finally say, lifting my head up to look at her, "where have you been and what on earth is the matter with you?" I push myself back up to sitting a bit. "We've been so worried about you."

I don't say, "And here's Paul. We ran away from home and took a bus all the way to Florida and we've come to break you out," because that might rush things a tidge. So Paul just stands behind me quietly without an introduction. Waiting. He's had to do a lot of that today.

"Oh, Ivy," Mama says again. And then she says, "It is a long story, baby. I am so, so sorry. About everything. I'm fine, though, now. I promise you I am. I needed to get my blood pressure under control. I was having fainting spells. I thought they were due to all my upset over that scoundrel of a man I was fool enough to follow down here, but really it was just my blood pressure acting up. I forgot my medicines at home." She pulls herself up onto her elbow as she talks, which makes her look more like her normal self than she did lying flat on her back. "That scoundrel of a man" is Hallelujah Dave, I guess, and it doesn't sound like she's too fond of him anymore. Which seems like a minor miracle, if you ask me.

I hurry to pull Mama's bottles of pills out of my backpack and set them on the bed beside her. "Here. I brought them to you. But I guess I'm a little late."

Mama looks down at the pills, and she doesn't look back up at me. She starts talking in this really low, slow way. "Oh, Ivy. Oh, you dear, dear heart. It doesn't matter, baby. I got what I needed right here. I'm really perfectly healthy now. I think I'm only still in the hospital because I haven't gotten up the courage to come on home, so help me heavenly Father, and I had nowhere else to go."

Without turning her head to look up at me, she reaches to touch the gold cross at *her* neck, the one Daddy gave her for their tenth anniversary when she passed her old one down to me. They're nearly the same, only this one's real gold, through and through.

"All your life I've tried to set a good example for you, baby." She holds on to the cross as she talks. "And now I'm just so embarrassed, really too embarrassed to make my way back to y'all. I failed you, and I failed your daddy, too. I—" She stops suddenly and leans up higher and looks around. Her eyes are wide and worried. They flutter, flutter, flutter, and finally find me again. "Ivy, where *is* your daddy?"

And I know this sounds sillier than a girl my age has any right to be, but I wasn't expecting that question. It catches me straight up, and my breath hooks a little in my chest.

"He is, um . . . well . . . Daddy isn't here. He didn't come."

Mama pops all the way up now, and she swings her legs over the side of the bed so she's facing me and looking very much like my mama again.

"What do you mean he didn't come? Where is he and how did you get here, Ivy Green?"

My breath hooks again, and I truly can't tell if anything's going to come out of my mouth when I open it. "On the bus," I say. And that's it. That's all I say. That's all that comes out.

"The bus? You came to Florida on the bus? Alone, or with Daddy?"

"No, ma'am. She didn't come alone. She came with me." Paul's voice, clear and strong, comes from behind me. Thank goodness.

I squeeze my hands onto my knees, to remind myself and make absolutely certain that I *am* here, sitting solidly in this chair instead of floating. And then I turn my head slowly to look up at Paul.

"She came with *you*?" asks Mama. "What in heaven's name? You're Paul Dobbs, isn't that right?" Mama sounds like she's just this very moment noticed Paul standing in the room with us, which seems, no offense, kind of clueless.

"Yes, ma'am," says Paul.

"Okay, well. Mercy. And aren't *you* lucky to be right smack dab in the middle of this family drama," Mama says. And then she actually laughs a little, in a tired sort of way.

"Mama, I wanted to find you," I say, turning back toward her and reaching out to hold her hand again. "And Paul was willing to help. It's not that far on the bus, honestly, and here we are. We found you, and you're okay. So. That's that."

Only, that *isn't* that. Not at all. Because we're still trapped in a hospital room in the panhandle of Florida, and Daddy's on his way to rescue us right now. If he finds us here, I'm no better than Mama, needing to be hauled home, and that is *not* how I'm going to finish this whole thing. I'm gonna succeed. I'm gonna get it right. Mama's flopped back on the bed again, only her legs are still hanging over the side, so everything looks kind of dislocated. And she shuts her eyes in a headachy grimace. It looks like we're a long way from right.

"Mama, really," I say. "We're gonna go home now and this'll all be over. Daddy's gonna be glad to have us back!" I think about Paul saying the very same thing to me, and I cannot tell you how much and deeply I hope that it's true.

"This is all my fault, Ivy. You don't need to make excuses. My twelve-year-old daughter took a bus to Florida, alone. Well, not quite alone, Paul, but you know what I mean. All on account of me. Good God in heaven, what hath I wrought?"

Which is a Bibley way of saying "What have I done?"

There's a little three-knock rap on the door, and I have never been so relieved to be interrupted in all my life. Another nurse—not Nan—comes in. She is towering tall and her eyes are very bright. "I am sorry to interrupt this happy powwow," she says, "but I need to grab your vitals, Ms. Green."

"Kids, this is Raquel," says Mama, and she sticks out her arm for the blood pressure cuff without being asked. I realize as I watch her that Mama's got a whole little life going on down here. Hallelujah Dave and The Great Good Bible Church. Nan and Raquel. Blood pressure cuffs and hospital food. A whole little life I know nothing about at all. She's been gone that long.

Raquel chitchats with us while she takes Mama's blood pressure and pulse and temperature, makes notes on a chart at the head of the bed, and moves over to crank open the window a bit.

"Alrighty, friends," she says. "I'll leave you to it. And I don't see why you can't head home soon, m'dear," she says to Mama. "You're doing very well, and now your family's here. We'll see if we can get the doctor to clear you tomorrow morning."

Which, with Daddy hot on our trail, is not soon enough for us. And it doesn't take much to convince Mama that we owe it to everyone to hustle up and head on home.

When we sneak out of the hospital forty-five minutes later, Mama leaves a note that reads:

To Whom It May Concern—
I'm sorry I had to check out rather suddenly.
Thank you for the fine care you've given me.
I'm feeling much better. Here is my home
address in Loomer, Texas, in case you need that.
God bless you and keep you in his care.
Diana Green, patient
2203 Magpie Lane
Loomer, TX 78972

That's the thing about Mama. She can sometimes be kind of freakily polite. I mean, who on God's green earth leaves a thank-you note and a forwarding address when they're running away?

I wish she would've done that when she ran away from us.

The plan is this:

We sneak Mama from the hospital.

We rent a car.

We call Daddy and Mr. and Mrs. Dobbs from the car to tell them we're okay.

We start driving west toward Texas.

Pretty simple.

But the part about the phone calls? That part is

Mama's idea. It was all I could do to stop her from calling Daddy right then and there in the hospital. I reminded her that we were kind of trying to be quick about getting out of there and getting home. I *didn't* tell her that if we waited much longer, Daddy was gonna do the getting home for us. I know Daddy's worried, I do. And he's probably halfway to Florida already. But I don't want to call. Neither does Paul. We were just getting used to keeping to ourselves, if you know what I mean. "Flying under the radar," Paul calls it. And if I'm gonna be more than an idea girl, I need to stay under the radar and finish what we started.

But I can't see a way around making the calls eventually. Mama is worried Daddy may never forgive her. Those are the exact words she used, and she wants to start making things right as quick as she can. Which makes me worry all over again that Hallelujah Dave might have been some sort of boyfriend to Mama. A bad boyfriend, but still . . . Daddy can't be any too thrilled about that.

"So here's how I see things," says Mama standing at the rental car counter waiting for the agent to find us a car. "We'll start driving this afternoon, but we won't make it all the way home tonight. With God as my witness, I plan to deliver you both to Loomer in one solid piece, not a scratch on you. Falling asleep at the wheel won't do at all."

"Yep. Understood, Mrs. Green," says Paul. He stands right beside Mama, holding her suitcase upright. There's something about the way it's packed that makes it want to tip over, so Mama's given Paul the job of keeping it propped up.

"Safe and sound, that's what I promise you both. But that means we'll need to stop for the night somewhere along the way. At least we can get a motel room. Anything should be better than that bus y'all rode down on, right?" She taps her credit card against the counter as she talks, like she's nervous. Maybe because she and Daddy try to save it for emergencies, so I guess this is kind of an emergency.

"Yep," says Paul again, keeping up our end of the conversation as I stand, half-asleep, right behind him. I feel like that bus we rode down on is catching up with me. And the jail. And the hospital. The whole thing is catching up with me, really. I yawn with my eyes closed.

"I've got a nice Chevy Malibu for you," says the agent lady to Mama, and as Mama turns her attention to the paperwork, that's when it hits me. Hard.

I've been so concerned with finding Mama and keeping ahead of Daddy that I'm about to let us head straight home to Texas without so much as mentioning the space shuttle or Cape Canaveral, Florida.

Chapter Seventeen

I want to call Paul's parents first, to put off talking to Daddy just a hair longer, but Mama says, "No, honey. It's time. We need to let him know that we're all okay, and that I'm well and good and responsible for you again. Now that I'm out of that hospital, I have the strength to do what's right."

She doesn't ask *me* if *I* have the strength, so I'm guessing that doesn't affect her decision one way or the other.

We're in our rental car but haven't even started it up yet. Mama and I are up front, Paul is in the backseat with the map we got inside, and for the first time in a long time, things feel kind of settled. But still. I feel a little pang at giving over the phone. I can tell as soon as Mama starts to dial that she's fully in charge again, and I'm back to being a plain old twelve-year-old from an itty-bitty town in east Texas.

It's funny, really. Ever since Mama left, I've been missing her hot-cooked breakfasts and dinners, and her happy laugh, and just plain her. But I've also been babysitting and going to church and doing my best to take care of Daddy while he did his best to take care of me.

And somewhere in there I made friends with Paul, and we made some actual plans out of our ideas, and we ran away to Florida, of all things. For an adventure—that's what we've been having! Paul was right about that, and it suddenly seems so much bigger and more important than having to eat cold cereal for breakfast every now and again.

"It's ringing," Mama says. She's got her index finger pressed against her brow, which means, *I am in the middle of something right now. Please don't disturb me.* So I don't. I don't say a thing.

Mama sucks in a quick breath and then says, "No, it's not Ivy. It's Diana. It's me." So I know that Daddy has picked up the phone. There's a long pause—Mama's listening, I guess—and then she says, "Oh, mercy. We do not need the whole entire family racing to the state of Florida, Maxwell Green. I am fine. I'm here and Ivy's here and Paul's here. We are all fine, and you should turn yourself right around and drive straight back home to Loomer. We'll be there before too long."

I turn around to see what Paul's up to, to see if he's listening or not. His head tilts toward the map opened on his lap, but when he looks up at me, I mouth the words "space shuttle" silently. Paul just kind of shrugs and smiles. And then I hear Mama's voice start to quiver, so I turn back around.

"I know it, Max, and I'm sorry. I'm so sorry. It's a big mess, and it's entirely my fault. I can't tell you how sorry I am that I ever left at all. I'm going to make things right with you. And with Ivy. We are going to talk it through on our way home and . . . What? . . . Yes. Yes. You can talk to her. And, Max, I love you." Mama hands the phone to me, which is a good thing, because now I'm mortally embarrassed at having Paul sitting in the backseat overhearing every little thing my Mama and Daddy have to say to each other. (But, also, I'm pretty glad about the "I love you" part.)

"Hey, Daddy," I say.

"Ives. I'm so relieved. I've been so worried. I'm pulled over on the side of the highway right now, and, man, I'm just so relieved, I can't even tell you."

And here's something funny: *I'm* suddenly relieved too. All this time, ignoring Daddy's phone calls, I forgot how safe he makes me feel. I was afraid of him, when really, I needed him. He gives good advice and good hugs, and I think I get now why he didn't want to go chasing after Mama and Hallelujah Dave. That could be pretty embarrassing if it didn't work out. It'd be like Paul showing up at NASA expecting to sign on to a space shuttle that didn't exist anymore.

"Oh, Daddy, me too," I say. "But Mama's right. We're fine. And I'm sorry I scared you. That wasn't the point. The point was to find Mama, and we did that. Do you know that, Daddy, that that was the point?" I see Mama, out of the corner of my left eye, slump over the steering wheel. I turn to look at her straight on, to make sure that she's okay, but I can't tell. Her forehead's on the wheel, and her shoulders shake.

Still, as sad as it is to see Mama crumble, I decide to tend to Daddy, since he didn't really have anything to do with any of this from the start. And he tended to me all summer, pretty well, if you think about it.

"You still there, baby?" he asks.

"Yep. I'm still here. And I really am sorry, Daddy. We both are, both Mama and me."

And it's true. I am sorry. Or at least, I'm sorry that I worried him. I don't truly know if I'm sorry that I came.

"Honey, I made a big mistake," Daddy says, "not taking all your worries about your mama seriously. I had no idea you were upset enough to board a bus to Florida, for

God's sake. For God's sake, Ivy!" His voice gets a little louder as he goes on.

"I know it, Daddy. You were doing your best. But so was I. This was my best, Daddy. And now we've got Mama, and Mama's got her pills, and everything's fine. We're gonna be home before too long. Okay?"

I feel Mama shift in the seat next to me, and the next thing you know, she's starting up the car. "Paul," she says quietly over her shoulder, "shout out if you see a good place to eat. We've got to ready ourselves for the long drive home."

So. I guess we're on our way.

"Daddy? Listen. I have to go. We still need to call Mr. and Mrs. Dobbs and then, y'know, help Mama with directions and all."

"Right. Thanks for the call, baby," he says. "I feel so much better. But I still really wish you hadn't run away, sweetheart, really." And then he does a sort of sigh that has both a laugh and a cry in it. It sounds like some combination of relief and fear and disappointment and disbelief. Like he's thinking, *Out of all the people on God's green earth, we've never been the kind of family who'd get wrapped up in a thing like this. Any of this!*

"I know it, Daddy. I really do know it." And then I can't

help myself, I just say it. "Parts of it have actually been a little fun. I mean, not the scaring you part, but . . . it's been an adventure!"

Mama pulls out of the parking lot, and Daddy starts to laugh for real. Hard. A big, rolling Daddy laugh. It takes him a second before he can even answer me. "Fun?" he says. "I've got the Loomer police on speed dial and I'm halfway through Louisiana with my pedal to the metal, and you're having fun? I think the Greens have all gone officially crazy. Don't tell your mother I said that, Ivy, but sheesh."

And then he keeps on laughing, only not in a way that seems totally funny. So I tell him I love him, and he says he loves me back, and we hang up. But even still, I picture him sitting there in his truck, laughing and laughing on the side of the highway in that not very funny way.

Mama exits when she sees a sign for Applebee's, and says, "I can't imagine what you two have been eating, but I know I've been living on Jell-O. I think we need to start this trip off with something hot and good and real." Both Paul and I moan with relief.

"But, Mrs. Green," says Paul, "I'm afraid to say we're

just about broke. We had some, umm, trouble with money on the way down here." Which you have to admit is an especially nice way to put it, considering it was really *me* who had the trouble.

"Oh, honey," says Mama, "you don't know the half of it. I don't have two dimes to rub together, thanks to Davey Floyd, and sending him to the county jail isn't going to fix that. So. We do our best." And she smiles.

Which I know means, *We use the credit card again.* Emergencies are starting to feel not so bad after all.

"Bring the map in with you," she says as she shuts off the car. And it appears that she's so frazzled from talking to Daddy that she's forgotten Paul needs to make a call too. But Paul doesn't mention that.

We settle into a booth and order—a burger for me, club sandwiches for Mama and Paul, chocolate shakes all around—and Mama says, "Okay, let's make our route. Paul, honey, do you want to find Loomer for us?"

Paul does as Mama asks. We all have to move our waters aside so he can spread the map out on the table. We sit silently for a few seconds while he smoothes it out and takes a look.

"The problem," he says, "is that Florida and Texas are both so big, and there's a couple of states in between here and there." He flips the folds back and forth, sticking fingers in between the sections to hold his place, and tracing the lines of highways, working his way west, trying to get us to a hotel before dark.

"No, hang on a second. Wait!" I say, a little louder than I planned. "Wait! That isn't the problem!"

Both Paul and Mama jump a little, like I've startled them, and they look at me, confused.

"The problem isn't that Florida and Texas are big. It's that we shouldn't be headed toward Texas at all," I say.

Paul's eyes open wide as Os. I can see that he knows what I'm getting at. He looks kind of horrified. And then he kicks me under the table. Hard. My shin buzzes and stings.

"What in heaven's name are you talking about, Ivy?" asks Mama.

"Um, nothing," says Paul, his cheeks all purply red. He shakes his head, just barely, at me.

"Yeah, never mind," I agree. "Nothing." I pull my foot up onto the bench next to me and rub my leg. Sheesh. Paul wanting to say good-bye to the space shuttle is *not* nothing, but I'm not gonna risk mortal injury turning it into something, I can tell you that right now.

We're back in the car, all full and fat and happy, before Mama suddenly remembers about calling Mr. and Mrs. Dobbs. So Paul calls. And here's something kind of crazy.

They are *not* on their way to Florida. They are not parked on the side of the highway halfway through Louisiana like Daddy was, and they're not at the airport or the police station or anywhere urgent at all. They're at home in Loomer, and their plan was to let Daddy pick up Paul and bring him home where he'd be "good and grounded for a long, hard time."

Apparently they tried to call Paul, but his phone was at home in his room, turned off. ("They'll catch us for sure if we bring phones," he said before we left. And, yep, he was right about that.) So since then, they've just been waiting, and "fuming," says Paul, which I happen to know from Mrs. Murray's vocab list has to do with being quietly angry.

Now that plans have changed, they've approved Mama as the driver instead of Daddy, and the time it takes us to get back to Loomer will be good, because it'll give Paul's dad "some time to cool down." That's what Mrs. Dobbs told Paul, that his dad had worked up quite a head of steam and Paul would be smart to let him cool down.

"What if we tell them that it's my fault?" I say, seeing as how, let's face it, it is. "Will that help?"

"No. Don't worry about it. It'll be fine," says Paul. "They're not really home enough to keep me grounded. They'll get over it."

I'm about to say, "But are they relieved, like you thought they'd be? That you're fine and everything?" But before I can, Paul hands the phone up to Mama and flops back in his seat with a big, tired sigh. Somehow I know not to say anything else.

Maybe this is what it means to be distinguished. You don't go racing after people when they run away, and you don't laugh-cry with relief when they're found. You just fume. Which is sort of sad, if you ask me. I mean, it's one thing to have worked up quite a head of steam—I guess my daddy did too—but here's Paul, alone in the backseat of a rental car, in the panhandle of Florida, for goodness' sake. The least they could do is laugh-cry, right?

We drive on quietly for a little while, and the next time I look back at Paul, still slumped down low behind me, well, that's just it. I can't stand not speaking up for another second.

"Mama, stop!" I shout. And before I've even figured out what else to say, Mama jams on the brakes and veers over to the side of the road.

"What? What?" She looks from side to side, all panicky.

"What, Ivy? *What* is the matter?" Like she's wondering if we almost had an accident with a car she hadn't seen.

I purposely look at Mama sort of sideways so I don't have to look at Paul, too. "We have to turn around, Mama. I'm sorry."

"Ivy . . . ," says Paul from the backseat, and I think, *This is why I'm not looking at you, so you can't stop me the way you did back in the booth at the restaurant.*

"Paul, wait," I say. "Mama? We have to go to Cape Canaveral. That's why Paul's even here in the first place. I mean, along with keeping me company while I looked for you. And I'm sorry I scared you, but this is really important. He's getting grounded for nothing if we don't make it to Cape Canaveral."

"Cape Canaveral? Florida?"

"Yes." I peek back toward Paul and lift my eyebrows in a sort of silent warning to just go along with me. Which feels a little funny, being bossy when I'm actually trying to be nice, but taking charge is all I can think of to do. "That's right," I say. "Cape Canaveral, Florida. Where the space shuttle lives," I say.

If we can just get Mama to say yes without too much discussion about how it's time to get home and how worried Daddy is and how Cape Canaveral is clear

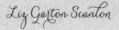

across Florida, we'll be fine. Once we're back on the road, I think she'll keep going just to be polite to Paul.

I guess Paul read my eyebrow warning right, because he says, "Yep, the space shuttle. We were hoping to go, but I mean . . ."

I can tell he's about to give in again—I can hear it in his voice—but I won't let him. Not this time. "You know how the space shuttles are retiring, Mama? Well, the idea was, since we were gonna be in Florida anyway, we would just sort of run on over there to see one. Or at least to see where they used to launch them. Or something."

"Oh my. Oh my goodness. This is a change of plans," says Mama. As if everything else we've been doing has been all plotted out. She sits with her hands on the wheel and looks out the window toward where we *were* going. Paul and I sit too, and wait.

"Well." Mama clears her throat. "I'm not exactly certain where Cape Canaveral is, so let's look it up on the map. And also, we'll need to get back in touch with Max, and with your mom and dad, Paul, before we set off to do another thing. Oh dear. Well, okay," she says.

Which, you have to admit, sounds an awful lot like yes.

"So if we find it on the map, and call home, then you're fine with it? Is that right, Mama?"

Mama's whole body shivers, and she reaches out to turn off the air-conditioning that's been blowing hard while we sit here in the sun. "Well," she says, "I didn't know a thing about this arrangement, but it seems only fair to you, Paul. And maybe it could be my way of making things up to the two of you. At least a little. After everything. Okay?"

Okay? Yes, yes, and amen yes. This is indeed okay, because I know my mama, and she will not go back on her word. She may have run off to Florida with a crooked preacher and forgotten her blood pressure medication and left behind her phone and scared us half to death, but she will always, no matter what, keep her word.

Even once she discovers where Cape Canaveral really is.

Chapter Eighteen

According to Paul, Mrs. Dobbs thinks a side trip to Cape Canaveral "sounds fine," which I'm pretty sure means she'll allow it because she's too distinguished to kick up a fuss. My mama doesn't say anything, but she does give Paul's hand a little squeeze when he gives her back her phone, and I love her for that.

I also love her for saying that she'll explain our detour to Daddy so I don't have to. Because honest to goodness, if I have to hear his laugh-cry one more time, I might give up completely on Cape Canaveral, even though it was originally my idea.

It's after we've worked everything out—Daddy, the map, the plan—and we're on the highway again but turned around the other way, that Paul says, out of the blue from the backseat, "Thanks, Ivy."

I'm about this close to saying, "Thanks for what?" when I look down at the map in my lap, with a new circle drawn around Cape Canaveral, and I nod.

"No problem," I say. And really, it isn't.

For the next couple of hours, Mama gets us to tell her every little thing about our "escapade." That's what she's calling our trip to Florida, an escapade. I think it's supposed to make all of us feel better. Which it does, and so does telling the story with Paul. We make it funnier than it was, even the fainting and throwing-up part, and the losing the money part, and the Skinny Ricky and Hallelujah Dave part. Mama actually laughs a lot, and so do we.

Paul compares our trip to one big experiment and says we were following the scientific method all the way along. Mama believes him. He makes it so that I practically believe him, even though I was there and I don't remember following any particular method at all.

When we stop to get gas, I go into the ladies' while Mama pumps and pays. And it's in that hot, tiny, hold-your-breath bathroom that I suddenly realize something: Mama has not told us one itty-bitty thing about her own summer or Hallelujah Dave or The Great Good Bible Church of Panhandle Florida. I've tried to turn the conversation her way a couple of times, but she keeps turning it back toward us. Which feels like a trick to me, like she's been trying to distract me the way she did when I was a fussy baby and she'd blow on the mobile hanging over the rocking chair.

That mobile stayed hung until we turned my room into Fluffy Pinksville in third grade, and by then it really *was* distracting—and babyish. And now this trip is starting to feel babyish too, with Mama not telling us anything important and acting like we didn't just make it all the way to Florida on our own. So by the time I get back into the car, I don't care how much I've missed her, or how sweet she's been to Paul, or how easy it was to get her to agree to Cape Canaveral; I'm mad.

"Okay, you little adventurers," says Mama as we're buckling in, "what do you say we turn on the radio and just ride for a while? The light's changing, and I need to focus on where we're going, which is a good piece farther than I realized."

She pops a piece of gum into her mouth, pushes the scan button on the radio, and puts the car in gear. And then, as she starts backing out, she mutters, "Sweet goodness and mercy, what will your daddy think when we finally make it home from all this?"

And for me, that's it.

That's just flat-out it.

"What will Daddy think? Really? What do you think

Daddy thought when you abandoned us to go gallivanting all over God's green earth with Hallelujah Dave? What do you think *I* thought when I showed up in Florida and discovered that there *was* no Great Good Bible Church? And that you were in the hospital? And that your fake preacher man with a bun in his hair was in jail?" I hear my voice, and I know it's mine, but it's as if it's gone ahead without me, as if it's motorized and spinning like one of those centrifuges in science class.

Mama stops the car completely, half in and half out of the parking spot, and she clicks the radio back to off. Her face goes all white—she looks worse than she looked when we arrived at the hospital this morning. And I don't care. Or maybe I do care but I can't stop anyway.

"You've been listening to us this whole entire drive so far, as if Paul and I have been away at summer camp or something. But this isn't summer camp, Mama! This is real life, and I left my babysitting job and lied to Daddy and got on a Greyhound bus to Florida, all because of you!"

It is eerily quiet in the car every time I take a breath between words. I think Mama and Paul are every bit as surprised as I am by the words coming out of my mouth.

"Do you know we've been worried about you, Mama?

Do you really know that? And that we missed you? Pastor Lou was right—you forsook us! You were supposed to be like Ruth, Mama, and stick with your family no matter what. That's supposed to be in your moral fiber. What about that, Mama? What do you have to say about that?" I feel the centrifuge in my throat slowing down as a lump moves in and tears fill my eyes.

But Mama? She just sits there, staring at me. She doesn't say a single thing.

"Mama, my God, I'm dead serious here! Wake up!" I shout through the lump and through the silence, and that's when her hand flies up to slap me.

I catch it, just as it's grazing my cheek. I feel a fingernail scratch my skin, and I watch her mouth fall open, like she's just done something she didn't know she was going to do.

"Oh, Ivy. Oh, angel. What in heaven's name is happening to us?" She moves her hand toward me again, more slowly this time, as if to pat or stroke me, but I push away from her, my back pressing against the door.

"I owe you a lot of explaining," she says. "I know I do. But I also know that I have never in my life heard you speak to me like that, or take the Lord's name in vain. We are good stock, and we don't do that, Ivy. It only makes things worse, and things are quite clearly bad enough already."

The car hums under us, and my cheek stings. My mama may have never heard me talk like that before, but she's never slapped me before either. Why is *she* the one who suddenly gets to be mad here? I feel my eyes, hot and heavy with the tears I do not want her to see. I can't stand it, not even for another second. I twist around and pull at the door handle and start to jump out of the car. Mama grabs on to my sweatshirt and then on to my actual shoulder.

"No," says Mama.

The car rolls backward a bit. Mama steps hard on the brake, and all of us jerk in our seats. I kick my feet out toward the pavement.

And suddenly Paul says, "Wait, Ivy. Stop. Stop!"

But I don't.

"You care more about a God you don't even know than you do about me!" I shout at Mama over my shoulder. And then I step out completely and slam the door with all my might.

Chapter Nineteen

I run hard across the parking lot, which turns into a bunch of other parking lots all strung together. I run past stores and salons and restaurants with their huge signs, and I run past shopping carts all lined up. I run past big concrete gardens of hard dirt and spiny-looking palm trees. I run past a little red car that has to stop for me because I don't stop for it.

I run and I run and I run, and while I run, I yell. I yell at Mama and at Hallelujah Dave. I yell at Daddy and at God and at Pastor Lou and at Paul. I run, and I yell. I pound out every angry thought I've ever had as I run and run and yell and yell and my eyes and my lungs and my insides burn. I keep on running even after there's nothing to yell about anymore. I keep on running until my breaths turn into gasps and the bottoms of my feet hurt and I reach the concrete wall that marks the end of all these parking lots.

And then I stop. I press my hands up to the concrete and I come to a lurching, gasping stop. I have no choice because from here there's nowhere else to go. I'm done running and done burning, and everything inside me suddenly tumbles down toward my feet, just plain crumbles, like a church turning to ash.

I don't have a money pouch. I don't have a phone. I don't have a map. And right now it really, truly feels like I don't have a mama.

My whole sweaty, tired body leans up against the retaining wall, and I close my eyes for a long time. It feels like almost forever, really, just standing here. Not yelling, not crying, not even thinking. The setting sun shines bright against my eyelids, and I feel itchy and puffy and red. And tired. I'm really, really tired.

When I finally open up my eyes, there is nothing to do but turn around and start the hot walk back to the car. And as I do, there's Paul, coming across the parking lot toward me. He moves slowly, like this is not an emergency at all, like everything is fine. And then do you know what he does? He lifts his hand and waves. Like we've just bumped into each other at the mall or something. Just a little wave, that for some reason makes me laugh. I wave back.

"I'm kind of stuck here, I guess. I mean, I can't really go anywhere. I don't have a phone or a ride or any money,"

I say when we're close enough to hear each other.

"Yeah, I know." Paul stops and turns around when I reach him, so he can walk with me.

"Sorry about all this," I say.

"I think it's really your mom who's sorry," says Paul. He swings his arm out in front of me to stop me from walking straight into a pickup truck. Once it passes, I see our rental car, on the other side of the gas station, parked at a weird angle with the driver's door hanging open.

"She's not acting very sorry."

"Yeah, I know," Paul says again.

As we get closer, I can see that Mama is not *in* the rental car. The door's hanging open, and I think the car is even running, but Mama's not there.

"Um, where is she?" I ask.

"Looking for you."

Paul and I wait in the car till Mama gets back. She's panting, like she ran as hard as I did. She's panting and red. She gets in and pulls shut the door.

"I'm so sorry, Ivy," she says. "So sorry." And then she pulls tight on the steering wheel, backs out of the parking space, and starts to drive.

She leans forward as if it's hard to see, never mind

that it's not dark yet and the window is clean. Paul is completely silent in the backseat, and I lean up against the door, as far away from everyone as I can possibly be, considering the fact that we're cooped up in a car together.

We drive for nearly an hour, but it feels twice that long without a word from anyone. Finally Mama says, "I know it's up to me to break the ice here, but I don't know where to start except by saying I'm sorry again."

Which does seem like the right place to start, but I don't say so.

"I made a lot of mistakes, Ivy, including slapping you. That's what people do. We make mistakes. Terrible, awful, stupid mistakes. And I've mixed you up in mine. I could talk you through everything, every crazy thought I've ever had and every stupid thing I've ever done, but no story will really fix it all."

I don't say "yes" or "okay" or "I know." I don't even turn her way. I've said everything I need to say. It's Mama's turn now.

"I hope you can forgive me sometime, Ivy. In the meantime I have to work on forgiving myself. And then it's up to God. That's the really awful thing about this whole mess— I was just trying to get closer to God, which makes it even a bigger shame that I messed up as badly as I did."

I still don't turn to look at her, but I listen. I think Paul's listening too.

I mean, really, what choice do we have?

Chapter Twenty

I spent my whole livelong life trying to be a good girl," says Mama. "But it didn't seem to help, or matter. Because every single Sunday of my childhood, no matter how good I'd been, my daddy would preach a sermon with the angry breath of God behind him. I knew that he *and* God were keeping tabs on me, and I was terrified of them both."

Terrified.

I feel a tiny crack open inside me, but not enough to turn her way.

"But then I grew up a little and I was blessed with your daddy, Ivy, the sweetest man who ever lived."

"Mmm-hmm," I say, 'cause I feel like I owe that to Daddy.

"And with you. You were a baby made in God's image if ever a baby was," Mama says. "I've had such a happy life with you both. It's like you washed away all the fire and fear that came before you."

She stares straight ahead and drives in her careful way

as she talks. She stops talking when a huge loud truck goes flying by, making our little car wobble and rattle in the wind. Mama's arms clench up tight till the shaking stops. And then she drives on, quietly. Really quietly. It makes me impatient.

"But if you were so happy with us, why did you leave?"

"I wish I could take that back, Ivy, I promise you."

Which, you'll notice, isn't an answer.

"There was something about those wildfires that just got me spinning straight out of control," she says. "When I learned that my daddy's church burned down, I felt so sad and so sorry, even though he'd been gone for years."

"You felt sorry for him? For Granddaddy? Even though he never felt sad or sorry for *you*?" I shift in my seat so I can actually *see* what she's thinking, not just hear it.

"You didn't know him, Ivy. He was a good man deep down. Really," Mama says, almost like she's scolding me. Never mind that all I've ever heard about Granddaddy is how loud and angry and scary he was. I play her words back over in my head to be sure she said what I think she said.

"Mama, pardon me, but that's crazy talk. He scared you and he made certain you were scared of God, too. How is that good at all?"

I turn back to look at Paul, for sympathy or confirmation or something. He looks a little horrified to be included. He stares at me without so much as a blink, so I turn back to Mama, waiting till she answers.

"Okay, honey, wait. We're getting off track," says Mama.

Off track? What track were we on? The Granddadddy's-suddenly-good-and-made-me-go-to-Florida track?

"For whatever reason, those fires made me miss my daddy—they just did—and missing him led me straight out to the Tomko Center, where Davey Floyd had set up his ministry. Davey was so familiar. His voice, his preaching . . . I got sucked straight in. I couldn't help it."

And as she says that, I remember something Paul said at the park one day, about his daddy telling him a career in space was "impractical." And how Paul said that *he* kinda thought it was impractical too, but he couldn't resist it anyway.

"Is that how it's been with you and space, Paul? Like you couldn't help yourself?" I ask. "Like no matter how impossible it seems, you just want to be a part of it anyway?"

Poor backseat Paul. I keep dragging him into the conversation, I guess because Mama's answers aren't very satisfying to me.

"Um . . . ," he says, but Mama doesn't give him a chance to finish.

"It's just that everything makes such perfect sense if you listen to Pastor Lou," says Mama. "Even *God* makes sense. Davey arrived and reminded me of the *other* parts of God—the fire and the anger, but the mystery and miracles, too. So, yeah, I guess that *is* a little bit like space, isn't it?"

I guess. But even if we're comparing God to space, I still don't get why Mama would leave us for it, or for him. And she doesn't say.

She just goes on about how Davey turned out to be a swindler and a stone-cold fake. (With a hair bun and glassy eyes, I think but don't say.) And about how the police came to shut down The Great Good Bible Church—which wasn't really any kind of church at all—and how she ended up in the hospital, so far from home.

"I was lying there feeling sorry for myself," says Mama, "when I thought of God in scripture, saying, 'Rise, pick up your bed, and go home.' Just like that. And in some crazy roundabout way, that's what I'm trying to do now. I've made everything so complicated, Ivy, when really, my only job is to love the people I've been given to love. My own daddy, for all his preaching, wasn't very good at that. But I am."

"Well," I say. And then I don't say another thing, because actually, this summer, she hasn't been very good at loving us at all.

After Mama finishes her quote-unquote "explanation," we drive on for hours without any of us uttering a single solitary word. It's fine for a while—a relief, really—but now it's pitch dark and the silence is starting to feel a little creepy. I wonder if I should turn on the radio. Or talk to Paul. Or maybe say a prayer.

Then I think about how Mama and Daddy didn't give me a middle name in order to leave room for God. Maybe that's what we're doing now. Leaving room for God. Or for one another. Or for that one clear voice Mrs. Murray told me about. Maybe.

Mama keeps driving, and it just keeps getting darker and darker and quieter and quieter. The truth is, that "leave room for God" explanation has never made me feel any better about my missing name, and it's not helping me feel better about this creepy quiet car, either.

Chapter Twenty-One

When you drive around this part of Florida, you can tell right away that the space program is a big deal. The newspaper they gave us at the hotel has a little orbit drawn around the O in "Today." There are signs everywhere for the Kennedy Space Center, and a restaurant called Planet House, and a Laundromat called Sonic Clean. There's even a street called Astronaut Boulevard. Honestly, it's like space is as important to the coast of Florida as God is to Loomer, Texas.

"Hey!" says Paul as we pass another billboard with the space shuttle on it. He points as it disappears behind us. "No way. Did y'all know they call this 'the Space Coast'? Man. How good does it get? I live in the wrong place, that's for sure."

I'm kind of awed that Paul would suddenly imagine himself up and moved to a place he hardly knows a thing about. I kind of want to defend Loomer, since it's not that bad a place to live, never mind that we *did* run away. Temporarily.

But I don't say anything about feeling awed *or* defensive, because I'm just relieved that somebody in this car is talking again. Driving across an entire state in almost total silence is harder than you'd think.

At the motel last night Mama and I each got a bed, and Paul slept on the floor. Which I thought was a mighty injustice, since Paul had been sleeping in cars and buses for three days, and Mama had been in a fancy motorized hospital bed with people bringing her soda pops and bendy straws.

But Paul is a gentleman, and he was not gonna take a bed from a lady. He actually said that. (Maybe Paul is a better example of distinguished than his dad, after all.)

This morning I flopped across the backseat of the rental car, still kind of sleepy, even though I had a bed of my own last night, and Paul sat up front with Mama. That's where he is now, straight and tall, looking out the front window and then the side one, and then the front one again, sort of vibrating. I know he's smiling his little half smile even though I can't really see it from back here.

"You're excited, aren't you?" I ask, and as I do, I feel almost a kind of jealousy. I don't know if I've ever loved or wanted anything as much as Paul loves and wants space.

I mean, a dog, maybe. But dogs are an ordinary thing to want and not quite the same as space. I guess I wanted Mama to come home pretty badly, but that was more like a necessary repair than a dream.

"Excited? Are you kidding? Of course. I mean, my dad took me to the Johnson Space Center in Houston a million years ago, because I drove him crazy begging and pleading. But then he talked the whole way there and back about what a long drive it was. Which is why I totally can't believe you did *this* long drive for me, Mrs. Green."

If you ask me, Paul is being nicer to Mama than she deserves, but I don't want to spoil his joy, so I let it be. Plus, he's right, it has been a pretty long drive. This morning we don't have an actual plan since we haven't exactly been on speaking terms, but Mama's following signs to the space center, which makes as much sense as anything else, it seems to me.

I pull myself up to look out the windows with Paul. It's flat as flat can be out there, but very pretty. I mean, if a town is surrounded by the ocean, of course it's pretty.

"So, Paul," says Mama, probably just glad that *some-one* is talking to her, "have you been interested in space forever and ever? I mean, since you were small?"

I realize I don't even know the answer to that, which might mean I'm not a very good friend. Ever since Paul and I started getting to know each other, I've been so caught up with Mama gone missing and all, I haven't asked him all the questions friends are supposed to ask.

"Yeah, always," says Paul. "I asked for a telescope when I was five. I didn't get it, though. My mom and dad gave me a pair of kid binoculars instead, with a picture of Woody Woodpecker on them. I don't think they quite got what I wanted to do."

"Parents often don't," says Mama.

Which is kind of an interesting thing for a parent to say.

"Paul was gonna be an astronaut, but then they decided to stop shooting off space shuttles, which ruined the whole plan," I say.

"Yeah. I mean, I don't know if I would've ever really gotten to fly," says Paul, "but, yeah . . ."

He's back to looking out the window, and I can see why. We have to cross another long bridge to get out to the space center, so we're sort of floating over a million gallons of salt water. There are gulls and grasses everywhere—it's like we're leaving the city and entering someplace wild. Not as in crazy wild but as in the actual wilderness. I wasn't expecting it to be like this, but maybe you need to be in the middle of nowhere if you're going to shoot stuff off.

'Cause then, right when you think there's nothing out here at all except for beach grass and birds, we see them. Straight ahead of us, growing up out of the earth like giant trees—rockets.

"Oh my God," says Paul.

"No kidding," I say, because honestly, it's pretty awesome-seeming so far.

What's not awesome is this:

Getting into the space center costs a fortune.

Maybe not an actual fortune, but considering that Paul and I have approximately zero dollars and zero cents left, from the hundreds of dollars we started with (thanks to whatever happened to me and my pouch back in Houston), and with Mama giving all her money to Hallelujah Dave, apparently. Well. It's a lot of money.

I think about Mama's credit card.

I think, *This is an emergency,* but I don't say it out loud.

We stand in front of the ticket booths, hot and dizzy. There are so many choices about which tours to do, and which sections to see, but none of them are cheap.

"I, um . . . I should've checked on this before we came. To see how much it cost," says Paul. "Wow. I'm sorry about this, y'all." He isn't vibrating anymore. People march past us to buy tickets, but we just stand with our hands in our pockets. Our empty pockets. I actually feel kind of empty through and through.

"Okay, so here's what we're going to do, gang," says Mama in a sunshiny Sunday school voice. "I'm pretty worn down after running out of the hospital like I did, and then making the long drive and everything. What I need to do is sit and have a coffee and spend some time on the phone with your daddy, Ivy. Being a tourist is too much for me today. It truly is. So the two of you will go on in, and we'll meet back here—"

"Wait, Mrs. Green. I don't—"

"No ifs, ands, or buts, Paul," says Mama, and away she goes to buy our tickets like a real, honest-to-goodness grown-up. Which is how we end up, just Paul and me, in the Shuttle Launch Experience, taking off.

We buckle into big roller-coastery seats that lean way back as the launch starts. It is windy and noisy, and the seats shake and buck and suck and press, and the miles fly by on the screen up front. My butt hurts and my back hurts and my head hurts, but I hold on to the shoulder railings and close my eyes and bump along.

And then? The next thing you know? We're flying. Floating. Our seats tilt forward. It is like gravity is gone and we are as far as you can imagine from anyplace we've ever known.

"Yes," says Paul, almost like a sigh. "This is awesome."

And then he says, "Wow."

'Cause there, right in front of us, is Earth, floating in a sky of stars. An Earth we're no longer on. It's enough to make you dizzy.

We walk out of the big tube that is supposed to be the space shuttle, and our fellow astronauts all seem as thrilled as Paul. I'm pretty sure I heard the words "dream come true" more than once. I'm glad for them, but wow, that's not exactly how I would put it. Once the crowd clears, I stop for a second to catch my breath.

"Okay," I say. "Well. It's official. I'm not gonna quit my day job."

Paul laughs. "Your day job, as in babysitting? Are you gonna be a babysitter forever?"

"Well, no. I'm not sure what I'm gonna be, but 'astronaut' has been officially crossed off the list, due to the fact that even a fake space launch made me both sick and scared."

"Sometimes scary can be exciting," says Paul.

"How do you know?" I ask. "You're not scared of anything!"

"Everyone's scared of something. I'm scared of dogs."

I'm about to accuse him of just trying to make me feel better, when I remember the dog at the bus stop in Tallahassee. I start to giggle. "All dogs," I say, "or just dogs in sweaters?"

Paul rolls his eyes and says, "Seriously. Are you gonna pick your career based on what you're scared of?"

"Well, no. I'll use a process of elimination, I guess, till I'm left with something I really like. And all I know right now is, no astronauting."

"'Process of elimination,' huh? If I didn't know you better, Ivy Green, I'd say you were being scientific." Paul's eyes twinkle, and his hair is all scruffled and he's back to that kind-of-cute look I noticed earlier. I don't know why—he's still in the same jeans and hoodie he's been wearing for days. Maybe it's just that he's happy.

"Ha! I don't think so," I say. "You sciencey guys are

all 'if, then' about everything, with your hypotheses and stuff. I always get stuck on the 'if' part."

I mean, honestly. I'm as likely to become a scientist as Paul is to become a preacher. I don't get around to saying that aloud, though, because a group of kids in matching purple T-shirts moves in between us, their guide walking backward as she talks.

"Space," says the guide, "is what we call the final frontier. But it's not called a frontier because we will move there and develop it someday, like we did in the American West, or even because we plan to visit, although we've done a little of that already. It's a frontier simply because it is the edge of what we know and understand. Space is a mystery that we want to know more about. When we look up at the stars, we notice their beauty, and we wonder about them. That's how all of our astronaut heroes began their journeys, you know—looking up at the stars and wondering, like you and I do."

I turn my head and look up. All the summer camp kids do too, even though it's daytime and we're inside. You just can't help it. And I don't know what Paul is thinking—unless he's wishing that he'd gotten to come to a camp like this when he was a little kid—but what *I'm* thinking is this:

Looking up at the sky and wondering is what science people like Paul do.

And it's what God people like Mama do too.

If that's not the craziest thing.

Chapter Twenty-Two

After looking at some cool displays and seeing a very 3-D IMAX movie (that makes me dizzier than the launch simulator did), Paul and I eat lunch in the cafeteria. We have to hurry because we have tickets to take a bus tour at one o'clock, which you must admit is kind of ridiculous, us getting back on a bus voluntarily after our Greyhound adventure. I think it officially qualifies us as good sports.

Lunch is expensive, so we split a kind of measly chicken sandwich to keep within Mama's emergency budget. I have a feeling that when we get home to Loomer, I may do nothing but eat for a whole week. Paul must be starving too, but he doesn't mention it, so neither do I.

"Y'know that thing we were talking about earlier, about hypotheses?" says Paul, passing me our small shared soda.

"No. What thing?" I look at the clock over Paul's head. I'm actually starting to worry a little bit about Mama. I may be mad at her for a whole list of reasons, but she is still my mama, and she is sitting out in the hot sun just one day after getting out of the hospital, for goodness' sake. Then I realize Paul is talking, and I shake my way back to him.

"Y'know, how you said you're just an 'if' person. I was thinking about that, and here's the thing. That's the part that scientists like too. That's the idea part. I'm pretty sure everybody likes the 'if' better than the 'then.' I mean, at least people who're adventurous—like us."

I look across the table at Paul with his sorry-looking sandwich and his bus tour wristband. He really is *so* happy, it's almost as if we got to come for a real launch. I don't have the heart to tell him that I'm just plain old Ivy Blank Green. I'm not really adventurous at all. Or at least, I'm only adventurous inside my head, not out of it.

When we get onto the bus, it turns out our summer camp friends are with us, but the counselor is sitting quietly because the bus driver is in charge now. He introduces himself as a "communicator," which is very sci-fi, don't you think?

When we make the first stop at the launch pad, lots of people get off.

"You wanna?" I ask Paul, since we've been told that

there are giant platforms out there and wild lights and other cool stuff.

"Nope," says Paul, kind of whispering under the communicator's instructions. "I'm good. I can get the idea from here. I'm holding out for *Atlantis*."

Because here's the thing. We are going to the Vehicle Assembly Building next, and guess what's in there waiting for us? Space Shuttle *Atlantis*. A real honest-to-goodness space shuttle, in person. It might be the very one that Paul would've flown himself someday, if the people in charge hadn't messed up his plans. And here it is, on display. If that's not the luckiest.

And now here we are. The bus stops. The door opens. Paul almost trips over me, he's in such a hurry to get out. We pass people headed in the other direction to get back on the bus, and most of them are looking at photos on their phones.

"You can't capture it," someone says as we walk by. "It's too spectacular."

It turns out they weren't just talking about the space shuttle. The building *itself* is spectacular. It's the biggest building you've ever seen. Light pours in from everywhere. Massive metal frames stretch up high like the Eiffel Tower. Forklifts and trucks rest on the concrete floor like tiny toys. And in the middle of it all, the space shuttle—a great big blown-up version of one of Paul's remote control planes, but this one is for real. Absolutely 100 percent real.

"*Atlantis* went to space thirty-three times," says the tour guide.

Thirty-three times! How did we not know that? Even in little Loomer, where we sometimes miss what's going on in the next town? Why wasn't it a bigger deal? Why wasn't it a big deal every single time?

"How in God's name could a person even imagine a thing like that?" I ask as we stare up at the wide white wings and American flags. "And then be brave enough to fly it? To space, of all places? I mean, is that brave or crazy?"

"Brave and crazy go together," says Paul, smiling, answering but not looking at me. His whole body buzzes; he's almost floating. He is what Pastor Lou would call awe-struck. And not that I would spread this around school or anything, but he looks this close to wanting to cry.

Brave and crazy. Brave and crazy. We were a little brave and crazy getting here, he and I. Never mind that Paul's afraid of dogs and I'm afraid of, gosh, almost everything *but* dogs! We were still both brave and crazy. And thank goodness, 'cause Paul has *This was worth it* written all over his kind-of-cute face.

"Right now we're looking at Space Shuttle *Atlantis*," says our guide, "but it's important to think about what came before the shuttles and what's coming next."

What came before, it turns out, were the Apollo rockets that flew to the moon. They were built right here.

"You could be standing in the very spot where Neil Armstrong once stood." The guide's voice bounces around. Paul looks down at his feet.

"Neil freaking Armstrong," Paul says.

"I know," I say.

"And before too long," says the guide, "our next generation of rockets will be built here. Ones that, someday, might take the next generation of astronaut explorers to Mars."

"Paul!" My voice comes out louder than I expect it to. Some of the people standing nearby turn to look at us, but I don't care. I grab on to his shoulder to make sure I have his attention. "Did you hear what he said?" I ask, in something a little closer to an inside voice. "He said 'next generation.' Did you hear him? That's you!"

And Paul Dobbs, astronaut-to-be, stands right there in Neil Armstrong's footprints, and starts to laugh.

"Huh," he says. "What do you know? Maybe space won't just be for robots and the rich." He shakes his head as the guide keeps talking about all the things they've got planned. "Maybe there's gonna be a spot for me after all, Ivy Green," says Paul, and he laughs and makes fists out of both of his hands and kind of pumps them up and down.

It's like our whole trip has been Paul's "if" and this, right here, is his "then." The "then" he didn't count on.

I can't think of anything to say except, "Don't give up," but that sounds kind of cheesy, so I don't. I just swallow hard. The guide keeps talking. Space Shuttle *Atlantis* hulks over us, huge and white. Paul's hands relax and hang by his sides.

When the formal talk is over, he shakes his head again. "Oh, man, Ivy. I'm an idiot. You know what I did? I got so into the space shuttle that I kind of forgot about space." He looks up at the shuttle, and then farther up, to the tip-top of this enormous building, like when we were with the camp kids earlier, inside. We're both just looking up and up and farther up, into the light and sky and space we know is out there.

"Wow," he says. "Dang." And he smiles.

And right then I see my mama in my head. This is

an awful lot like what happened to her, I think, following Hallelujah Dave to Florida as if he were God or the space shuttle or something. But it turned out that God isn't a preacher with weird blue eyes and a hair bun. God is really more like space. Big, wild, mysterious space.

Which I'm pretty sure is what Mama was looking for all along.

Chapter Twenty-Three

S o this is it. Tomorrow morning we're piling back into our rental car and heading west, straight toward home. But tonight we are on a beach at the edge of the Atlantic Ocean.

When we came out of the space center, Mama was waiting. She had on a new straw hat and was reading a magazine and drinking an ice tea.

"I knew you'd be in there a good long while," she said, "so I drove around and got myself a souvenir and found us a new hotel. One right on the beach. We deserve it."

"Can we afford it?" I asked, but honestly I was just relieved to see her smiling and not turned to a puddle on the pavement due to heatstroke.

"Baby doll, this is why we have a credit card, for these unforeseen circumstances," Mama said. "You let me worry about the details."

And so I do, because she *is* the mother, after all.

As we make our way toward the beach and the new hotel, Paul and I tell her about our day. I hope maybe she won't notice that I'm sort of casually talking to her again. Somehow my anger melted clean away between the time when she dropped us at the gate this morning and the time when she picked us up this afternoon, but I don't want to make a big deal out of it. I just want to enjoy this last bit of time before we have to go home and explain ourselves to everyone.

I do ask for her phone, though, so I can text Daddy as we drive. Not to explain anything, just to say hey. Because now that I'm not hiding from him, I'm missing him. And I can still see him pulled off on the side of the road in Louisiana, worrying up a storm.

R u home safe n sound, Daddy? I type. *We'll be there soon.*

And then I send a second one: *Luv u to the moon n back.*

I've hardly pressed send when a message comes back. *I love you double that. Love, Daddy.*

Isn't it funny how he signs his text like he's writing a letter, even though I obviously know who it's from? I guess he's more distinguished than Mama gives him credit for.

The hotel restaurant has round, red-glass candles on every table, and we eat shrimp cocktail and snapper for dinner because Mama says, "Far be it from me, kids, to give you something like pizza when we're sitting nearly smack dab in the center of the ocean. Far be it from me."

And then when we're done, we walk across the patio and kick off our shoes and step onto the beach. Which is where we are now, right down near the waves, the tiny foamy waves. We're lying with our knees bent and our backs against the sand, and the tiny foamy waves say *hush, hush, hush*.

On one side of me is my runaway Mama, who accidentally and unexpectedly brought us here.

And on the other side of me is certified science guy Paul Dobbs, who did too.

It's gotten dark and the stars have come up, and just a small, funny chunk of the moon.

We talked a lot over dinner, all three of us, and laughed about how I got all banged around in the launch simulator and am not—repeat, *not*—cut out for space.

And then Paul told Mama that there's totally gonna be a future for him in the space program after all. "I'm still a little bummed," he said, "but I think I got too obsessed with the space shuttle when it's just a machine."

As we finished eating, we kept talking like that, on and on. It was fun. We were finally not hungry and not tired and not mad at one another, and it seemed like there was so much to say.

But now, here on the beach? We're quiet as mice, until Mama says, "Darling Ivy. I'm so sorry, baby. I really truly am."

I can tell she means it, but it's so nice right here and now. I don't want to hash everything out—and I know that's what Mama's gonna say any minute now: "Let's hash this out."

So I just say, "It's okay, Mama. Really. Everything's fine. I get it."

"But I never should have left Loomer, honey. I never should've followed that ridiculous man to his fake church or forgotten my blood pressure meds or left you and your daddy behind. None of that ever, ever should have happened, and I'm sorry. I'm sorry to you and to your daddy, and to Paul, too."

"But, Mama," I say, pushing myself up to sitting, "if you hadn't done any of those things, then we wouldn't be here right now, lying on the beach and looking at the stars shine. Maybe sometimes the wrong things have to happen so the right things can."

"Oh, honey. You've always been good at making the right things happen. You didn't need me to go off half-dumb and crazy for that."

"But see, that's just it. I did! I did need it. I'm always full of ideas, but that's only the first step. You can have all the ideas in the world and still spend your life just stuck in one place."

Mama sits up too, but she doesn't answer. She just looks out at the water and the sky like I do.

Then after a while she says, "Y'know, Ivy, you were right. I forsook you and Max and my own heart and home. I lost faith in everything that was good. But, baby, *you* never gave up on anyone or anything. You stuck by your daddy all the way through this hot, hard summer, and by me when you decided to come all the way to Florida to find me, and by Paul, making sure he got this part of the trip, no matter what. I may have blown it, but you were steady, Ivy. All the way along."

Was I? Steady?

Steady like Ruth?

Is Mama right, about that and about me?

What if I love *people* like Paul loves space?

Before I have a chance to answer, she says, "And, Paul, I'm sorry you didn't get a full moon tonight. Or even

211

much of a moon at all. That hardly seems fair to a sky guy like you."

There is no answer, and for a second I think Paul may have fallen asleep. I lean over to check, and realize he's fine. Wide awake. Stargazing. He smiles a tiny quiet secret smile. At me. Ivy Ruth Green. I try this out on myself—this new name. This new middle name that means I'm complete. Steady. Loyal. Faithful. Maybe not in quite the way Pastor Lou would recommend, but in my own deep, true way.

Ivy Ruth Green.

My whole name, even though I didn't know it till today.

I hear it in my head, clear as a bell, just like Mrs. Murray said I would.

"Oh, don't worry about it, Mrs. Green," says Paul. "The moon's pretty, but it can get so big and bright that it drowns out everything else. Sometimes it's more interesting to stargaze when it's dark like this."

So that's what we do. We lie back and look at the stars—hundreds of thousands of stars, including that baby bear and his mother. After a while, Paul reaches over with his left hand and gives my right hand a squeeze, and then he just holds it and I hold back. It doesn't feel romantic; it just feels nice. And somehow I know that if Mama notices, she'll understand.

She'll understand that sometimes when you're looking up in wonder at the great-good heavens above, you are so full up with mystery and surprise that it feels nice to hold on to something that you really know.

Author's Note

Nearly every piece of this story is fictional, including the characters, their adventure, and the little town of Loomer, Texas. But the fires that set Ivy and Paul's great-good summer in motion were based on the all-too-real Bastrop County Complex fires that burned in September and October 2011.

Those blazes—born of a terrible and unlucky combination of drought, high winds, and record-breaking temperatures—killed two people, burned more than 1,600 homes to the ground, devastated beautiful old loblolly pine forests, and turned countless lives on end.

The fires in this book took place eight months after the Bastrop fires, but in my imagination they were very much the same in their catastrophic impact on both people and place.

Also shaped by reality was Paul's sorrow over the end of NASA's Space Shuttle program. After thirty years and 135 flights, NASA launched its last shuttle missions in 2011. The Space Shuttle Atlantis—the one Ivy and Paul would have seen during their visit to the Kennedy Space Center—bears the distinction of having made the final flight. It was the Space Shuttle Endeavour that flew piggyback on a 747 jumbo jet to its new home at the California Science Center in Los Angeles, the museum Paul referred to. It passed over central Texas in September 2012. From the church steps in Loomer, Ivy and Paul would have had quite a view.

Acknowledgments

Even fiction requires the generosity of experts. My friend Brian Anderson imparted both scientific and religious insight, something only a Renaissance man could do. Linda and Jerry Bernfeld were my eyes on the ground in Florida and at the John F. Kennedy Space Center. Tara Gonzalez provided Tallahassee tips, and Rachel Barry Hobson and Greg Leitich Smith offered their own NASA notes. Any misinterpretations of science, space, religion, or Florida are mine, in spite of this help.

I started this story on retreat at the Texas gulf coast, with friends to whom I'm ever grateful: Kathi Appelt, Anne Bustard, Rebecca Kai Dotlich, Jeanette Ingold, and Lindsey Lane. Early readers included my sister Chris, my niece Nina, and my daughter Willa, who read the whole thing aloud to me so I could hear it as a twelve-year-old might.

My critique partners—Anne, Lindsey, and Bethany—are each wise, wonderful, and in this book in many ways. I'm a lucky duck to have them. Likewise, the camaraderie of friends I've found within EMLA, Austin's SCBWI, my Poetry Sisters, and the Circle of Word Lovers.

Starry-eyed thanks to Allyn Johnston and Andrea Beebe Welch at Beach Lane Books, who, with laser focus and wicked intuition, bring out the best in me and in my work. Art director Lauren Rille delivered beauty beyond measure, and the whole Simon & Schuster team made this book better than it was when they got it.

Marla Frazee is one of the best creative partners in all the world. I love that we've been given this memorable glimpse of Ivy and Paul through her eyes.

And speaking of collaboration, this book wouldn't exist without Audrey Glassman Vernick. She's great-good in every way.

Erin Murphy, whom I call both agent and friend, is receptive, honest, and somehow both grounded and visionary—my own personal Hubble Space Telescope.

My family—including Pam and Rob Garton, Christina Garton Coppolillo, the Scanlon clan, and my beloved niece, nephews, aunts, uncles, and cousins—make up my favorite constellation.

And finally, thanks to my husband, Kirk, who is exceedingly tolerant and encouraging of me and my career. And you too, Finlay and Willa, are also tolerant and encouraging and the very reason I write for kids. You three are smack dab in the middle of my universe.

A Reading Group Guide to
The Great Good Summer

By Liz Garton Scanlon

Discussion Questions

1. Examine Ivy's motto that "Every good day starts with an idea." What does this mean? Why is it so important to her? What was Mama's reaction to hearing Ivy's motto? Does her response suggest Mama's general perspective on life?

2. Why does Ivy's mom run away with Hallelujah Dave? How does her absence affect Ivy and her father?

3. Compare Mama with Mrs. Murray. How are they different? Similar?

4. Explain what Ivy's dad meant when he said, "Church folks understand other church folks." Do church folks share common beliefs and ideas? How so? Since Mama is a member of the church, why are her actions misunderstood by everyone there?

5. Ivy says that her parents didn't give her a middle name because they wanted "to leave room for God." What does this mean?

6. Paul is interested in science and even wants to be an astronaut. Consider how scientific reasoning affects Paul's faith in God.

7. Explore the symbolism of the bus driver named Magdalena. Note that a woman named Mary Magdalene traveled with Jesus as one of his followers. Discuss other aspects of faith, mystery, and spirituality that serve as ties binding Ivy's story together.

8. Is Paul and Ivy's trip to Florida brave or crazy or both? Ivy refers to it as "a leap of faith." What do they have faith in, and is their faith rewarded?

9. Explain how Skinny Ricky is an unlikely candidate to lend assistance to Ivy and Paul. Why does he not seem to be the helping sort? Does he ultimately show another side of himself to Ivy? Do we know why?

10. How does Mama justify her reason for leaving with Hallelujah Dave? Could you forgive her, if you were Ivy?

11. Mama compares God to space, saying, "Davey arrived and reminded me of the *other* parts of God—the fire and the anger, but the mystery and miracles, too. So, yeah, I guess that *is* a little bit like space, isn't it?" How is space like God, according to Mama? Do you agree?

12. In the beginning, Ivy and Paul were classmates but not exactly friends. Why and how does that change? Are they as different from each other as they thought they were?

13. At the end of the book, Ivy renames herself. What does her name choice say about who she is and what she's learned about herself?

14. Discuss the issues of faith and forgiveness in *The Great Good Summer*. How did Ivy change and grow over the course of this book? What about Paul or Mama? Can you define and explain the story's theme, based on those changes?

Extension Activities

Musical Hymn

Look up the lyrics and music for the hymn "Blest Be the Tie That Binds." Listen, follow along with the words, and consider why this hymn was Mama's favorite. Write a short essay explaining how this hymn relates to Mama's character. What phrases in the hymn would Mama identify most with?

Star Study

In a short essay, compare and contrast the story of Ursa Major and Ursa Minor with Ivy and Mama's story. Describe the similarities between the two. List the ways that the stories differ. Is Paul right that the myths about constellations are a lot like stories from the Bible? How so?

This Reading Group Guide was created in concert with Debbie Gonzales.

debbiegonzales.com